THE CHRONICLES OF ETARFIA

THE SEVEN SISTERS

JULIA SMOLLIN

PublishAmerica
Baltimore

Softcover 9781462690886
PUBLISHED BY PUBLISHAMERICA, LLLP
www.publishamerica.com
Baltimore

Printed in the United States of America

Dedication:

I dedicate this book to all the important people in my life. They have always been there for me and I just want to thank you!

P.S: Almost all the characters in my book are based on real people!

ENJOY!

INDEX

The Beginning...9
Chapter 1 HULIONA.....................................11
Chapter 2 ELIANA..16
Chapter 3 HATARA.......................................19
Chapter 4 LATOPA.......................................22
Chapter 5 Rostoa...25
Chapter 6 Clerice..27
Chapter 7 Cira..30
Chapter 8 ICE, SNOW, AND MORE ICE........34
Chapter 9 FREE...39
Chapter 10 "WHO'S THERE?".......................45
Chapter 11 "WELL, I GUESS WE'RE GOING TO FRANCE." 47
Chapter 12 A GIRL NAMED CIRA................51
Chapter 13 THE TOUR..................................56
Chapter 14 MIRROR.....................................59
Chapter 15 SAFFERSTAR..............................67
Chapter 16 STORIES......................................70
Chapter 17 MISSING.....................................77
Chapter 18 KATRINA....................................79
Chapter 19 THE FIGHT.................................86
Chapter 20 THE MISTING MEMORY POOL..................88
Chapter 21 MIRACLE....................................91
Chapter 22 TAILS..93
Chapter 23 NO HOPE....................................96
Chapter 24 A CHOICE.................................100
Chapter 25 THE PALACE.............................106
Chapter 26 NATHLENE................................109
Chapter 27 TRAINING................................116
Chapter 28 WHO THEY ARE.......................126

CHAPTER 29 TRUTH..130
CHAPTER 30 GONE..136
CHAPTER 31 THWONK!...146
CHAPTER 32 THE PAIN OF BETRAYLE............................152
CHAPTER 33 BAD NEWS...162
CHAPTER 34 DAWN...179
CHAPTER 35 ONLY THE MOON...190
CHAPTER 36 THE SEVEN SISTERS.....................................213

NATURE

The wind is a song whistling by,
The trees are people standing high.
The grass is a carpet thrown on the earth,
The sky as blue as an ocean turf.

Flowers as tall as yard sticks,
Flowers as small as baby chicks.
Birds with feathers of yellow and gold,
Birds with black that are big and bold.

The mushrooms stand short and stout,
While tiny creatures scurry about.
Nature is a gift and we must treat it well,
For if we don't the world will be a story yet to tell…

By: Julia Smollin

The Beginning

Once upon a time seven baby girls were all born at the same time. But all were born in different parts of the world, Ireland, Greenland, China, Egypt, France, Canada, and Italy.

Their names were, Huliona, Eliana, Hatara, Latopa, Rostoa, Clerice, and Cira. It was very strange they were all born at the same time, for that had never happened before in the history of the world!

From the beginning they were destined to meet each other, but for now, they are oblivious to each others existence.

Chapter 1

HULIONA

The first was Huliona. She was born in Ireland, on the east coast. She lived on a Cliffside in a small white house, with a straw roof and a pathway made of cobble stones leading to the door. A little farther down near the cliff, in front of the house, there was a small forest with a river running through it.

Huliona was an only child. Sometimes she would secretly go to the river nearby and pretend to have a little sister. They would play house, cats, and even pretend to have magic powers. It was all fun and games for Huliona, until that fateful day, the day, that changed her life forever.

Huliona had been playing by the river as usual, but when she came home her father was sitting on the front stoop, silently. He had never been this quiet before. He usually greeted Huliona with a hug and a kiss, this time, nothing.

"Papa, what's wrong?" she stammered nervous.

"It's your mother," He said, looking up, his face, red from crying, his eyes sad. Huliona approached him cautiously.

"What happened?" She asked.

"She was coming home from the market, and…"

"And what?" Huliona said her eyes huge with concern.

"A raven flew down from a tree and spooked your mother's horse, it bucked her off its back," A tear rolled down his cheek.

"What happened?"Huliona asked again, already knowing the answer.

"She was hurt, very badly. The doctor, tried to save her, but he could not. Darling," He said taking Huliona's hands. "Your Mother has passed on."

"NO!!" Huliona screamed, "It can't be! I don't believe you!"

Huliona ran through the house in a frantic frenzy calling for her mother, but she never did get an answer.

Huliona was only seven years old when this happened. She did not know what she would do! Her Mother had taught her everything; she couldn't even imagine life without her! But, she did get by. For years she did her chores, and the chores her mother had done. In the meantime, Huliona's father raised her as best he could. He did not always raise her well, working full time, but Huliona knew he was trying.

By the time Huliona was thirteen the money was running extremely low, there was no work to be done. Her father could not find a job, no matter how hard he looked. His last resort was to work on a fishing ship, far out into the North Atlantic Ocean. He could not bring Huliona along, so he decided to send her to France, to live with her uncle for a while until he earned enough money to get the small family back on their feet.

SIX YEARS LATER

"But Papa! I don't want to go!" Huliona whined.
"You must."
"Why? Can't I just go fishing with you?"

"No! I already told you this, you are going to live with your uncle, and that's final! Now go pack!"

Huliona scowled. "Oh, Fine!" She slammed the door as she entered her room.

"Ey yi yi!" Her father said.

Huliona grabbed her small suitcase out of her closet. She stuffed what little clothing and possessions she had into it. Huliona zipped her suitcase up and lugged it out of her bedroom.

"Are you ready?" her father asked.

"Yes." Huliona said coldly.

"Okay, let's go."

Huliona followed her father out the door and over to the small mangled car in the dirt driveway. She climbed in, setting her suitcase on the floor next to her.

"Where does Uncle live again?" Huliona asked as her father as he stuck the key in the ignition and the car started.

"France." Her father answered.

"Oh." Huliona scowled in the front seat. "I've only met uncle a few times, how am I supposed to live with him for months?"

"I know." Her father answered. "But he is still your uncle, even if you don't visit a lot, and he cares for you. Things will go just fine."

Huliona's last attempt to try and change her fathers mind had failed. Utterly annoyed and disappointed, Huliona turned away from her father as they started for the dock. There was a deafening silence in the car. Huliona stared out the window at the trees zipping by. She longed to climb one of them and hang from its branches. She loved the rough feel of the bark under her fingers, the leaves brushing across her face.

"You will like your uncle's house, it is huge, and you can even choose your own room. And I heard from one source or another, that there is a surprise waiting for you."

"I don't care." Huliona said flatly.

"Listen, I know you don't want to go, but its for the best."

"How do you know? You could make almost no money fishing! You have no idea what they will be paying you!" Huliona replied, angrily.

"I know enough." Her father said in a wavering tone.

The car pulled into the dirt parking lot in front of the dock. Huliona opened the car door and got out. She grabbed her suitcase with a flourish and slammed the car door shut. She walked next to her father over to the wooden platform of the dock.

"Come on, you don't want to miss the boat!" Her father said jokingly, walking slightly ahead of her.

Huliona did not even crack a smile. When she reached the platform a man took her suitcase and brought it onto the ferry.

Huliona looked around, avoiding her father's gaze.

"Goodbye Papa." She finally managed to say.

"Goodbye darling, now be careful and do what your uncle says."

"Fine." Huliona sputtered.

"Huliona, are you okay?" Her father asked.

"No! What do you think?" She sobbed. Huliona's eyes filled with tears, she brushed them away with the back of her hand.

Her father pulled her into his arms.

"I'll just miss you so much!" Huliona wailed.

"I will miss you too," Huliona's father said pulling her back at arms length, his eyes tearing up. "But you know how much we need this money."

"I know."

"Miss," the Captain of the ferry said. "It is time to board."

"Go on now." Huliona's father said.

Huliona climbed onto the ferry. The captain then got on and pulled the loading plank onto the ferry, and closed the gate. The ferry started pulling away.

"Bye Papa!" Huliona called. "I love you!"

"I love you too!" Huliona's father called back.

Huliona's voice was soon drowned out by the waves, so Huliona's father did not hear the last thing she said to him, "Mother will watch over you!"

And with that, Huliona was off to France.

Chapter 2

ELIANA

The second sister is Eliana. Eliana and her brother Aden were born in southern Greenland, in a small town called Tingmiarmiut. Eliana was extremely young when her parents died, only five years old in fact, and Aden was only three. Her parents worked on a large fishing boat called the Two Lands. They were scheduled to go out for an overnight trip. When the boat did not come back for the night no one was worried, it was not until the next morning when the Two Lands did not return that people started to get anxious. The Two Lands was supposed to return at 6:00 but it did not. The people at port said that the boat was delayed because of the storm coming in off the coast. But, around ten o'clock, a search party was sent out.

The search party returned two hours later, with horrid news, and two people that were on the fishing boat with them.

To spare confusion, Eliana's aunt told Eliana and her brother what had happened to their parents when they were older. What happened was this, the boat was almost back to the port early that morning, and it was earlier than expected, so much so that everyone was in high spirits, laughing, talking, and not checking the <u>Two Lands'</u> computer. They did not see the "unexpected" storm on the radar. The storm drove the boat into jagged ice sticking out of the water. Only two people had survived, (they were not Eliana's parents), the rest had drown.

Eliana didn't miss her parents because she never really knew them. But she would often stop what she was doing and try to remember something about them. She remembered blurred visions, and muffled voices. She often scolded herself, frustrated that she could not remember. But life did go on. After her parent's death she and Aden moved in with their aunt and uncle. Eliana and Aden lived with them for the next eight years. When Eliana was thirteen and Aden was ten they moved into the house next door.

EIGHT YEARS LATER

"Aden! Hurry up!" Eliana shouted.

It was around six o'clock p.m Eliana and her brother Aden were packing all their things in boxes and suitcases. They were moving next door to their aunt and uncle. It was an exciting day for them. Eliana and Aden had been waiting for this for months! When Eliana came out of her room she saw Aden shove his stuffed polar bear into a suitcase then zip it up.

"Ready?"

"Yeah."

"Ok, let's go."

Eliana and Aden lugged their things outside and into their new house.

"OH! Aden, isn't it wonderful?" Eliana cried.

The house had three rooms, a living room, kitchen, and bathroom. There was no furniture, so the house looked stark and barren. The walls were a very light blue, almost white, and there was a skylight in the living room.

"Yeah, sure, I guess." Aden exlaimed. He was not the expressive type.

The two spent the next few hours unpacking. They didn't get their beds set up that day so they rolled their sleeping bags out on the living room floor.

"Aden! time for bed!" Eliana called.

"Coming!" Aden called back.

Aden walked into the room and slipped into his sleeping bag.

"Can we go exploring tomorrow?" Aden asked. Exploring was one of Aden's favorite things to do.

"Absolutely." Eliana said.

"YES!"

"But for now let's get some sleep."

"Okay. Goodnight Eliana."

"Goodnight Aden."

Chapter 3

HATARA

Hatara was born in western China. Both her mother and father were scientists and they were on a dig in China while Hatara's mother was pregnant with her. Hatara's mother was almost due, so when she started to have contractions on the dig sight Hatara's parents knew they were going to have their baby girl in China.

Hatara also had two brothers, Thor and Mathias. Thor was her older brother and Mathias was her younger brother.

Hatara grew up loving science as did her brothers. By the time she was eight years old she could pass the high-school science mid-term! By the time she was thirteen, she had to take a more advanced science tests than anyone in her grade. Hatara was also skilled in math and the arts; she loved to draw, letting her imagination take flight.

Hatara loved all her hobbies, but she really wanted to be a scientist just like her parents. She loved going on digs and expeditions with them. So far she had visited China, Antarctica, Spain, Scotland, America, England, Mongolia, Somalia, and South Africa. This time she was going to Greenland.

ON THE WAY TO GREENLAND

"Is the car all loaded?" Hatara's mother called.

"Yep!"Hatara called back.

"Dad, where's my CD player?" Mathias asked.

"It's in the trunk."

"Okay!"

A Few minutes later everyone was in the car, putting their seat belts on and rearranging themselves to get comfortable. They all packed fast and were ready in no time. The family was used to it because they went on so many trips.

"Everyone ready? Hatara's mother asked.

"Yep."

"UHU."

"Definitely."

"Okay, let's go." Hatara's father started up the car and headed for the airport.

"Now when we get to the airport I want you to get your coats ready for when we get off the plane. It's not a very long flight."

"Yes, Mom, we will." Hatara said.

Hatara and her family arrived at the airport in only a couple of minutes. They lived close to it because of all the traveling they did. Hatara and her brothers pulled their coats out of their suitcases. Hatara put her coat under her arm and jumped out of the car.

"Come on guys." Hatara said as she hurried after her parents.

The five of them boarded the plane. They walked down the aisle, avoiding people who were standing up, putting suitcases in over head compartments. They soon found their seats and sat down. They sat there for at least fifteen minutes, Hatara took out a book. Her brothers fiddled with their iPods and

CD players. Her father took out a newspaper and here mother closed her eyes to rest.

Suddenly a large whoosh was heard throughout the plane. Hatara looked out her window and saw that the plane was moving at lightning speed down the runway. Hatara loved flying, it was so exiting.

A moment later the plane lifted into the air. They flew over some trees then lifted higher into the sky above the clouds.

"I hope it's not too cold in Greenland." Hatara said.

"Well," her mother answered, opening her eyes. "I can't promise that." And with that said, Hatara and her family were off to Greenland.

Chapter 4

LATOPA

Latopa was born in western Egypt. She had a mother, father and one brother, Athos. Latopa's father had been ill for as long as she could remember, and her family had been poor for as long as she could remember as well. Latopa had no idea who her ancestors had been, so she did not know how her family had become poor. But Latopa did not complain.

Latopa and her family lived in a fairly large tattered tent near the Nile River. It had four sides and a pyramid shaped roof. Her mother and father shared a bed and Latopa and Athos shared a bed. They only owned the beds, a fire pit, and an old trunk with clothes and a few family jewels, too precious to give up or sell.

But one day, Latopa would loose what little she already had. Her life was going to change forever.

****

It was early morning when the first shot was heard, a scream, a yell, the sound of hoof beats across the sand dunes. Latopa was up and out of bed in two seconds flat.

"MAMA!" Latopa cried. "What is happening?!"

At that moment, men with swords and guns slashed through the tent. They bared their teeth in savage grins, and scanned the tent with hungry eyes.

Latopa's mother screamed. One of the men ran forward and dragged her out of bed. Athos ran to her aid. The man just tossed him aside, pushing him into another man who grabbed him and held him tight.

"Latopa!" her mother yelled. "RUN!"

The last thing Latopa saw before she ran from the tent was her father. He was kicked out of bed and dragged towards the door. His body weak and frail, not able to fight back, not able to protect his family.

"Latopa!" her mother yelled.

Latopa sprinted from the tent. She ran hard against the sand dunes. With the warmth of the sun beating down on her back. Latopa heard hoof beats behind her. She turned and saw men on horses thundering after her.

"NO!" Latopa yelled as she ran. She leaped over sand dunes and avoided gnarled trees.

Latopa saw the Nile ahead of her. If she jumped in, she might escape. As she neared the river, Latopa took the chance, and jumped. The world seemed to stop, everything around her went quiet. All she could hear was the rushing of the water around her ears. Suddenly, a strong hand reached into the river and grabbed her.

Latopa sputtered for breath as she was lifted out of the Nile.

"Thought you could get away did you?" The man holding her boomed. "Stupid child!"

He threw her onto his horse, and then climbed on. The horse's fur stuck to Latopa's wet body and her hair was plastered against her face. The dessert air choked her, making breathing hard. The horse thundered back the way they had come.

When they reached Latopa's tent. Her parents and brother were in shackles. A man then slapped a pair on her. The metal was hot, constricting.

"Come on!" one of the men shouted. "We need to get back to the ship."

The citizens of the Nile the men had captured, including Latopa, trudged across the sand. They were heading for the ocean, some to their doom. The sand stung the captives ankles as the wind picked up and tossed it around their legs.

Hot tears ran down Latopa's cheeks. But, little did she know, help was on the way.

<u>Chapter 5</u>

ROSTOA

Rostoa was a quiet girl. She lived with her uncle in France and spent most of her time in his huge library. She read all types of books, mystery books, magical books, history books, ect. Rostoa also loved to draw. She mostly liked to draw people, dragons and fairies. She usually hung the best pictures around her room and in the library. Rostoa loved to be creative, it was in her nature.

Rostoa had never really known her parents. She had often asked her uncle about them but he didn't like to talk about them. The subject seemed to unsettle him. Rostoa's uncle would retract into himself and often disappear into his study and stay there for quite sometime.

So Rostoa was pretty much alone, not knowing who she was or where she came from. But she had learned to accept it, keeping in mind the hope that she would one day find answers.

****

One day, in late afternoon, Rostoa was sitting in the library reading her favorite book, *Into The Mountains,* when her uncle walked in.

"Rostoa," he said. "I have wonderful news."

"What is it Uncle?"

"Your cousin Huliona is coming to visit."

"Uuu, I have a cousin Huliona?" Rostoa asked.

"Oh yes," Rostoa's uncle laughed. "I did not tell you about her yet."

So Rostoa's uncle proceeded to tell her about Huliona.

He told Rostoa that Huliona lived in Ireland and was going to come live with them for a while because her family was losing money. Her father had to work on a fishing boat to earn more.

"Oh! We are going to have so much fun!" Rostoa cried. "When will she get here?"

"In two days." Her uncle replied.

"I can't wait!"

"I'm glad."Rostoa's uncle said smiling, he then left the library.

"I wonder if I should make her a gift?" Rostoa said to herself. "I will." she decided. Rostoa had never really had a good friend, let alone any family to visit near by besides her uncle and she wanted to make a good impression on Huliona.

Rostoa went outside. She was going to make a fairy house for Huliona. She walked over to the big acorn tree near the edge of her woods. Rostoa picked up some acorns.

"These will work perfectly." She said.

The rest of the day Rostoa walked around her gigantic yard looking for things to put in the fairy house. She found things from pine cones to twigs to bark, and even a few small toad stools.

"I hope she likes it." Rostoa said, gathering the last of her materials.

"I'm sure she will." A voice said behind her.

Chapter 6

CLERICE

Clerice Winthro sat in her bedroom listening to classical music while combing her hair.

"I wonder what I'm getting for my birthday." She muttered.

Clerice was turning thirteen on June 19th, which was only two days away! She was psyched! She was going to be a teenager and her little sister wasn't.

Clerice and her family lived in Quebec Canada. They lived in a big blue house in a quiet part of their neighborhood, away from all the noise. For Clerice and her sister Christie's birthdays their parents always had something special for them, and Clerice was dying to know what her present would be this year.

A minute after Clerice had put her comb down her parents walked in. They had excited looks on their faces.

"Clerice," her mother said. "we have a surprise for you!"

"What is it!? What is it!?" Clerice cried, bursting with excitement.

"For your birthday we are going to take you to…" there was a brief pause. "France!"

"AHHHHHHHH!!!!!" Clerice screamed.

Christie could hear her from downstairs and covered her ears.

"No way!!!" Clerice cried.

"Yes way!" her father answered.

"When are we leaving?" Clerice asked.

"Tonight!" her mother said.

"Way cool!" Clerice cried.

"You better start packing your bags." her Father said. "We are leaving for the airport at eight o'clock sharp."

"I will pack my behind off!" Clerice cried with excitement.

"Well," her mother said "Get to it!"

Clerice ran to her closet and got her suitcase. She took all of her clothes and dumped them into it. She took shampoo, soap and her electric hair dryer. The last thing she put in was her stuffed rabbit Tuffey. Clerice took him on all the trips she went on.

"You'll be comfortable in here." She said, closing the lid of her suitcase.

When Clerice went outside her parents and Christie were already putting suitcases in the trunk of the car. There were quite a few, all stacked on top of eachother.

"Hurry up." Clerice's mother said as she took Clerice's suitcase and put it in the car. Soon they were all in the blue minivan.

"Ready?" Clerice's father asked.

"Yep."

"UHU."

"Ready." Everyone said.

Then they started to pull out of the driveway.

It only took thirty minutes to get to the airport. Clerice lived very close to it. When they arrived, Clerice and her family took their things and hurried over to the plane. It was the biggest plane Clerice had ever seen. It was white with a blue stripe all along the side and on the blue stripe *Mirical Flights* was written.

"Ticket's please." The man at the bottom of the planes stairs said.

"Here you are." Clerice's father said handing the man four tickets.

"You are in row two seats forty, forty-one, forty-two, and forty-three. Go on in." the man said.

"Thanks." Christie said.

Clerice elbowed her in the ribs.

"Ow!! What was that for?" Christie cried.

"You just don't say that!" Clerice said. "It's embarrassing."

Christie rolled her eyes and followed Clerice onto the plane.

Once on the plane, Clerice and her family put their things in the overhead compartments and sat down. Chrisrie put her ear phones in, Clerice's father took out a crossword puzzle and her mother grabbed her book from her purse, and Clerice gazed out the window.

"Please remain in your seats and buckle your seatbelts as the plane takes off." a nice lady voice on the intercom said.

"You heard her girls," Clerice's mother said. "buckle up."

"I'm so excited!" Clerice said.

"Me too." Her sister exclaimed, taking one ear bud out.

A moment later the plane rattled and shook, then it started to speed down the runway. When it got to the very end it took off into the air.

Chapter 7

CIRA

"Mom!!" Cira called. "Jathor and Carzon are annoying me while I'm trying to pack!"

"Boy's! Get out of Cira's room!" Cira's mother said.

Cira was packing for the family vacation she was going on. Cira and her family were going to France, one of their favorite places. They were not taking a plane, but driving. Cira and her family lived right on the border of France and Italy.

Cira lived on a vinyard. Her parents grew grapes to make wine. They had the best grape farm in their city in fact. Cira and her family were going on the vacation to celebrate all the good grapes they had grown that year. They were lucky; there had been too much rain, almost killing all the grape vines, but theirs had survived.

All of Cira's family was ready to go. Cira quickly put her silver iPod in her pocket, closed her suitcase and ran outside. She was the first one to get out to the car. She opened its trunk and put her suitcase in next to the folding beach chairs. She then opened the car door and sat in her seat.

"Come on guys!" Cira yelled from the backseat of the car.

"We're coming we're coming!" Cira heard her father yell from the house.

A few minutes later her parents and two brothers were putting their things in the trunk. Then once they were in the car Cira's mother started going over the list of things they would need on the drive.

"Water."

"Check." Cira said.

"Mini first aid kit."

"Check."

"Snacks."

"Check."

"Books."

"Check."

"Games."

"Check."

"Blankets."

"And check."

"Okay, we are ready to go." Cira's mother said.

A moment later Cira's father started down the driveway.

They were on the road for less than five minutes when Jathor asked, "Hey Cira, want to play a game?"

"No." Cira answered.

"Please!" Jathor pleaded.

"No! It's probably one of your stupid five year old games."

"Fine!" Jathor said. "But I have one more thing to say."

"What?"

"You're an idiot!"

"Do you want to tussle!?" Cira yelled.

"Bring it on!" Jathor cried.

Cira lunged for her brother.

Cira's mother turned around in her seat and yelled, "Look! It's only an hour drive! Can you two control yourselves until after we get out of the car!?"

"Yes." Cira and Jathor said quietly.

Carzon burst out with laughter. When her mother wasn't looking Cira slapped him in the back of the head.

****

An hour later they arrived in France. Cira and her family pulled into the driveway of a nice hotel. Everyone got out, stiff and tired. They all stretched before they went in. A minute later they entered the hotel and checked in.

"What room do we have?" Carzon asked as Cira and her family climbed the hotel stairs.

"Number twenty." His father answered.

The family climbed the hotel stairs to room number twenty. When everyone was in the room they picked their beds. Cira picked the queen sized one over looking the ocean. The sun was also the brightest there. She loved to be woken up by the sun shining on her face; it was a wonderful way to start the day, with the sunrise. She started to unpack her suitcase.

"Hey," Cira's father said. "Does anyone want to go to the beach?"

"Oh yes!"

"Totally!"

"Let's go!"

So, everyone changed into their bathing suits, grabbed their towels, and headed for the beach. They took a short walk down a side street then turned and cut through a park. A minute later they arrived at the beach. Cira and her family went strait down to the shoreline and spread out their towels. Jathor and Carzon grabbed their goggles from the beach bag and plunged into the water. Cira was about to join them when a small brown dot off to the right caught her eye. She squinted; it looked like a small boat.

"Hey mom," she said. "There is a small boat over there; can I go check it out?"

"Sure," Cira's mother answered. "Just don't go too far."

Cira took off along the shore line, the water lapping at her ankles. Thoughts of buried treasure and portals to other worlds whirled through her head. Whenever something like this happened to someone, she thought, those things always seemed to be thrown into the mix.

When she reached the boat she was out of breath and leaned against its side. But what was in the boat made her breath stop all together. Cira peered into the boat, stunned. Two girls, about her age were asleep in the bottom of the boat. But the strangest thing was that one girl looked Irish and the other looked Egyptian.

"What in the world..." she said

At that moment, one of the girls opened her eyes.

Chapter 8

ICE, SNOW, AND MORE ICE

Hatara sat in a ball huddled in front of a fire in the middle of the small village her family was staying at. She grumbled as another gust of wind blew snow in her face. So far, out of all the trips she took, this was the worst.

"I I ddon't llike GGGreenland!" she told her brothers, who were also as miserable as she was. "Esssspecially in wwwinter!"

"I I ssecondd that!" Mathias replied.

"I'm going to get a snack." Thor said, standing up.

He turned and headed for the village store. It was a small village, only a few houses. The common had the General store, a gas station, and a doctors office.

"Come on Mathias." Hatara said. "We should eat too."

Hatara and Mathias hurried after their brother.

It was very quiet in the small store. The only people there were the store clerk, Hatara and her brothers, and a girl about Hatara's age with her brother.

"I wonder if there are crunch bars here." Hatara said heading for the candy.

"Eliana!" Aden said. "Look! There are other kids."

Eliana looked up from the book she was holding and over to the other side of the store.

"Whoa!" she said. "I wonder why they would want to come here."

It was strange there were other kids, because, no one came to Greenland unless they had to. At least that's what Eliana's Aunt had said. They wouldn't come to Eliana's village either, since it was so small.

"Should we go over to them?" Aden asked.

"Sure." Eliana said.

Eliana and Aden walked over to the girl and two boys.

"Hi," Eliana said. "I'm Eliana."

"And I'm Aden."

"Oh, hi! I'm Hatara. These are my brothers, Thor and Mathias." Hatara said motioning to the two boys standing next to her.

"Hi." Hatara's brothers said.

"Are you new here?" Eliana asked.

"Yes. Our parents are scientists and they are here studying some old fossils frozen in the ice."

"Cool!" Aden said.

"Yeah, its fun at first, but it gets kinda boring." Hatara said.

"Hey," Eliana said. "Aden and I are going exploring, wanna come?"

"Sure!" Hatara said.

"No thanks." Mathias said. "Thor and I are helping mom and dad."

"Can I come?" Aden asked. "That sounds really cool!"

"Sure, mom and dad would love the extra help." Thor said.

Aden said goodbye to Eliana and Hatara, the three boys then ran out of the store.

"Well, I guess it's just you and me." Eliana said.

"Let's go." Hatara said.

The two left the store. They were greeted by a gust of wind and snow, but they headed out anyway.

"I didn't know there was anywhere to explore in Greenland." Hatara told Eliana.

Eliana laughed. "No," she said. "There is. There is this huge ice block down by the waters edge that you can slide down."

"That sounds like fun." Hatara said.

The two girls reached the ice block in no time.

"Wow!! This ice block is huge!" Hatara exclaimed, leaning against it.

"I know isn't it?" Eliana said. "Aden and I come here all the time."

Eliana grabbed onto it and started to climb up the back of the ice block, Hatara followed. The two reached the top.

"The view is really amazing from up here." Eliana told Hatara.

"You can see almost half of Greenland!" Hatara exclaimed.

Eliana laughed. "You probably are seeing half of Greenland."

Eliana then turned and sat down in front of the part of the ice block that looked like a slide.

"Woooohoo!!" she cried as she slid across the ice.

Hatara went next. "Ahhhhh!" She yelled as she slid down.

"That was so much fun!" Hatara said.

"I know! That was the best," Eliana stopped short.

There was a loud thud. The ice shook beneath them. The ice then started to crack, but they were small cracks curving in and out of the ice. Hatara and Eliana looked at each other, wide eyed.

"What's happening?" Hatara asked.

At that moment Eliana yelled, "GET OFF THE ICE!" as a huge leopard seal crashed through.

Both girls screamed, jumped up, and started running across the ice, the leopard seal following.

"I heard the fish population is down in Antarctica!" Eliana screamed as they ran. "It must have come here looking for food! This is unheard of!"

"It's gonna eat us!" Hatara cried.

"If we don't get away!"

A minute later Hatara slipped on a chunk of ice in front of her and fell. Eliana toppled over her. They slid across the ice right up to the waters edge. Eliana and Hatara reeled back in horror as the leopard seal reared up, ready to strike. As the seals head came down the girls rolled in opposite directions. The impact of the seals jaws hitting the ice was enough to crack it. The piece of ice Eliana and Hatara were sitting on turned into a block of ice. The girls clutched the ice block in terror as they were hurled out onto the ocean. The wave from the ice hitting the water carried them far from the land.

The seals mouth was bloody and had obviously received a serious injury. Seeing what had happened the seal did not follow them, but slipped back into the water, with one last bellow it disappeared.

Hatara and Eliana sat huddled on the ice block, not daring to move. They were shaking uncontrollably. Their clothes were wet and their noses red. They scanned the water for any signs of movement beneath the ice block.

"Wha, what should we do?" Eliana sobbed.

"We should call for help." Hatara answered, wiping tears from her eyes.

Then the two started to call for help. They called and called until their throats were sore. But the wind picked up and the ice block drifted farther and farther out to sea.

Chapter 9

FREE

Latopa sat, huddled in the corner of the slave ship she had roughly been thrown onto the day before. Her parents were gone, so was her brother, they had been put on a different ship. Latopa had mourned that day and she was still mourning now, as she sat on the tossing, turning ship. She shifted, trying to get her hands into a more comfortable position, the hand cuffs dug into her wrists.

Latopa decided to get up and walk around, she hoped it would get her mind off her family, (not that it would help much) she missed them a lot. She walked over to the side of the boat and looked over the railing. A dolphin was playing in a kelp bed. She laughed as the dolphin threw a piece of kelp in the air then caught it again.

"Hello dolphin!" she said.

Then to her astonishment the dolphin said "Hello Latopa!" and dove into the waves.

Latopa was so surprised she almost fell over board. But a man grabbed her by the back of her dress and threw her to the ground.

"What do you think your doing!" he yelled. "We need to sell you at the auction!" He stormed away.

"Sorry!" Latopa uttered sarcastically. Then Latopa stuck her tongue out at him when his back was turned.

Latopa then got up and went to sit on a bench nearby. She was confused. Could that dolphin really have talked to her? She didn't know, but she was determined to find out.

****

Huliona sat at the front of the ferry working on a quilt for her father. She had been on the ferry for a day and a night. She was almost to France and was worried of what her uncle would think of her. "Ow!" Huliona pricked her finger on her needle. She put her finger in her mouth. She stood up to try and find a bandaid. Huliona then noticed another ship in the distance. The ship was getting closer and closer, advancing more and more every second. It didn't look friendly.

"Captain!?" Huliona called. "Captain!!?"

"Yes, yes, what is it Huliona?" The captain answered as he came over.

"Captain, there's a ship over there. Its getting closer and it doesn't look, well, friendly."

The Captain looked over the water to where Huliona was pointing. He saw the ship and froze.

"Captain," Huliona said hesitantly. "What is it?"

The captain turned to Huliona. "Huliona get below deck right now." He said in an urgent tone. The Captain turned to leave.

"But why?" Huliona asked.

"Huliona get below deck right now!" Huliona then knew by the captain's sharp tone that the ship was not friendly at all.

Huliona grabbed her quilt and ran below deck. She heard the captain barking orders to the crew.

"Men," he said. "I never thought we would encounter pirates."

When Huliona heard this she almost fainted. She had heard countless stories about pirates capturing ships and holding hostages.

"But," the captain said. "I have done the math, and we cannot out run them, so, guns at ready!"

Huliona ran to the darkest corner in the small cabin below deck she could find, there she waited, stricken with fear.

Suddenly there was a loud thud.

"The pirates must be here!" her mind screamed.

There was another thud and then, shooting, shouting. There were splashes in the water. Huliona stifled a scream. She started to pull herself together and tried to think clearly. She couldn't just sit here! She had to do something! Huliona stood up and started to search for a weapon. She grabbed a knife out of the small kitchen. Huliona ran for the stairs. Just as she was about to go up, she saw another girl on the stairs. She looked about her age, and strangely enough she looked Egyptian. Their eyes locked.

Huliona then noticed the girl's hands, they were handcuffed. She knew this girl had to be a prisoner. Without thinking Huliona grabbed the girl's hand and pulled her below deck into a corner.

"Do you speak English?" she asked. The girl nodded obviously terrified. "Who are you?" Huliona whispered.

"I'm Latopa." the girl said. "I'm a prisoner on the other ship! I came here to try and find something to get these handcuffs off!"

"Okay, okay, quiet down. I'm Huliona. I was already on this ship, I'm heading for France."

"We really need to get out of here!" Latopa said

"I know, but the only way out of here is a small dingy." Huliona said. The two looked at each other.

"Let's go for it!" they said together.

First Huliona got Latopa's hand cuffs off by smashing the key hole with a hammer she had found in the kitchen. Then they each found a weapon. Huliona her kitchen knife and Latopa a hand gun she had found in a drawer.

"You ready?" Latopa asked.

"Ready." Huliona said.

The two girls crept towards the stairs, once at the bottom they rushed up. Above was mass chaos. There were people fighting everywhere.

"The dingy is on the other side of the boat!" Huliona yelled over the noise.

"Let's go!" Latopa shouted as she bravely shot at an advancing man.

Huliona and Latopa ran across the boat, dodging men with guns and knives. Many turned in confusion at seeing two girls caught up in this fight.

"We're almost there!" Huliona cried as the small dingy came into view. "We're gonna make it Latopa."

But just as the two girls reached the ladder that led down to the dingy a hand grabbed Latopa's dress and a hand grabbed Huliona's shirt and pulled them backwards. They landed with a thud on the floor of the boat.

"Your dead meat!" a husky voice said.

Huliona and Latopa looked up. A big, evil, gross, looking man stood in front of them, blocking the way to the ladder. Huliona's heart sank to her toes.

Sea foam sprayed up onto the deck of the boat, bringing with it bits of sea grass, and kelp. The sea grass went everywhere, causing some of the pirates to slip. A small piece landed on Huliona's head then fell into her lap. Suddenly Huliona felt a surge of power run through her as she sat there, looking at the sea grass. She picked it up and rubbed it in between her fingers. Then green sparkles started to fly around the sea grass. The sea grass twisted and turned and finally formed into a ring, a small green band with a sparkling green jewel set in the front of it.

"She's a witch!" the man shouted, his eyes wild. "She's a witch!" The man then brought his sword down, down, down.

Just before the blade hit Huliona, Latopa jumped up and ran at the man. With all her strength Latopa butted the man in the side, sending him toppling to the ground.

"Come on!" Latopa cried. Huliona shoved the ring on her finger and followed Latopa to the ladder.

"Thanks!" Huliona told Latopa as they climbed down.

"No problem." Latopa answered.

Once in the dingy Huliona started to saw at the rope that held it to the ferry.

"Come on, come on..." Huliona said as she sawed at the rope. It slowly started to fray. The rope finally gave. Latopa and Huliona each grabbed an oar and started to row. At that moment the dolphin that had talked to Latopa in the kelp bed came into view, and it had another dolphin with it. The two dolphins swam up to the dingy.

"Latopa," the kelp dolphin said. "You and Huliona will never get away paddling like that."

"Yes, let us help." The other dolphin said.

"What!" Latopa cried. "It's you again! How can I understand you?"

"You can understand those dolphins?!" Huliona asked, amazed.

"Yes, they want to help us get away." Latopa answered.

"Tell them to go in the direction of France." Huliona said.

Latopa told the dolphins this.

"Right!" the kelp dolphin said. "Let's go!"

The two dolphins then swam to opposite sides of the boat so it was wedged between them. Then they started swimming. As the boat was skimming across the water the dolphin's headed in the direction of France.

"This has been the weirdest day of my whole life!" Huliona said.

"Tell me about it!" Latopa answered.

Chapter 10

"WHO'S THERE?"

Rostoa whirled around. No one was there; the only sound was the rustling of the trees and a few birds in the garden.

"Who's there?" She asked.

Not a sound was heard.

Frightened Rostoa called "Uncle? Is that you?"

"No." a voice answered.

"Ahh!" Rostoa screamed, surprised.

"Do not be afraid." the voice said. "I have a message for you Rostoa."

"Wait!" Rostoa called. "First of all who are you? And what are you doing in my yard!?"

"You already know me." the voice said.

"But…"

"My message to you is this, Etarfia is in danger."

"What's Etarfia?" Rostoa asked.

"Tell the others." the voice added.

"Who are the others!?" Rostoa asked.

"You will know them when you see them." The voice said.

"Hello? Are you still there?" Rostoa said. But the voice had gone.

Rostoa ran back into the mansion. She ran down the hall and into the library. Once in the library Rostoa slammed its doors shut. She then ran to her favorite chair and sat down, shaking.

"What's Etarfia? Who are the others?" She thought. All these thoughts whirled in her head as she sat, in the huge library.

Chapter 11

"WELL, I GUESS WE'RE GOING TO FRANCE."

Hatara woke with a start. She saw she was still on the ice block. Hatara and Eliana had been on the ice block for two days. They were hungry and cold and no one had come to their aid. They were now out in the middle of the ocean on an ice block that would soon melt. Hatara looked over at Eliana, she was still asleep.

Hatara heaved a big sigh. The ice block moved. The ice block didn't move like it drifted across the water a few inches, but skimmed across the water like a boat. Hatara stared at the ice block, wide eyed. Hatara tried again, this time the ice block shot across the water, full force. Hatara laughed as she hung onto the ice block. But when she stopped blowing the ice block stopped moving.

"Eliana!" Hatara cried. "Eliana!" Hatara shook Eliana awake.

"What, what?!" Eliana said, sitting up.

"Okay, you're not going to believe me if I tell you so I'm going to show you."

Hatara took in a huge breath and blew out. The ice block shot across the water. Hatara stopped blowing. When she looked over at Eliana, Eliana was staring at her, her mouth hanging open.

"How did you do that?" Eliana asked.

"I don't know. I was just taking deep breaths and blowing out." Hatara answered.

"Here, let me try." Eliana said. Eliana breathed in and blew out really hard. Nothing happened. "I guess only you can do it." Eliana concluded.

"But I don't get it!" Hatara said, exasperated. "It's so strange!"

"Yah, it is pretty creepy." Eliana agreed as she stuck her hand in the water and twirled it around.

Eliana pulled her hand out of the water, she gasped. The water didn't drip off her hand. The water droplets stayed on her hand in perfect form! Eliana looked at Hatara.

"Try shaking it." Hatara suggested.

Eliana tried this. She shook her hand as hard as she could, but the water droplets only jiggled.

"Okay, now I'm getting scared." Eliana said.

"Yah me," Hatara started to say but then stopped; she was staring at Eliana's arm. Eliana looked at her arm.

"What the!" she cried as the water droplets formed four words on her arm, LOOK TO THE RIGHT.

The two girls looked to the right and saw a ship heading straight for them. As the ship got closer they saw the words, DAWSON'S TRADING CO. printed on the side of it. The girls stared, hardly believing their eyes. This had been the strangest day. The ship was literally right next to them before it stopped.

"Hey!" they heard a voice yell from the ship.

The girls looked up and saw a tall man standing on the ships deck.

"We're going to come and get you in our dingy. So hold on!"

"Okay!" Hatara yelled, now utterly confused.

Within minutes the men were next to the rapidly melting ice block helping Hatara and Eliana into the dingy with them.

"Thanks." Eliana said as she sat down.

"Oh, no problem!" the man who had called to them said. "Hey, how did you kids get out here anyway?" He asked.

"Uh," Hatara said. "It's a long story."

"But we are from Greenland." Eliana said.

"Wow!! You are a ways from home!" the man exclaimed.

"Why, where are we?" Hatara asked.

So, the man told them his name was Rick, and that he worked for Dawson's Trading Co., a company that traded with France.

"So, we're heading for France, we're actually only a couple miles from it."

The two girls went pale.

"Oh my gosh!" Hatara cried. "We couldn't have drifted that far!"

"Yes, you must have made a mistake!" Eliana said.

"Um, no, I'm sure I'm right." Rick said.

"You have to take us home!!" Hatara cried.

"Look, I'm sorry, but the only place I can drop you girls off is France." Rick said apologetically.

"But, but," Eliana stammered.

"Well," Hatara interrupted. "I guess we're going to France."

A minute later they were at the large trading boat, climbing up a rope latter to the deck.

"Hey, Hatara," Eliana whispered.

"Yes?"

"I know for a fact we could not have drifted that far."

"Well obviously we did." Hatara said. "What else could have happened?"

"I think," Eliana said "that when you blew us across the water, you actually blew us a couple of miles instead of a couple of feet."

"Oh, well we were going pretty fast." Hatara said. "That probably is what happened."

"I know it is." Eliana said.

Chapter 12

A GIRL NAMED CIRA

Latopa and Huliona had been in the dingy for days, with no food and no water. After the dolphins had gotten them on the right track they had left them. All the girls could do now was hope they would end up in France.

Latopa was sleeping. Huliona was awake, but did not open her eyes. Her back hurt, the dingy floor was very lumpy. Huliona tried to move onto her side, but then she noticed something, she could not feel the boat rocking back and forth on the waves. This caused her eyes to open. When she did Huliona saw a girl staring down at her from above, and it wasn't Latopa.

"Who are you?" the girl asked. "and what are you doing in this boat?"

Sudden realization kicked in. Huliona shot up; she saw she was on a sandy beach. The girl, surprised, fell over and landed in the water.

"Did we make it?" Huliona asked, excited.

"Make it to where?" the girl asked.

"France!" Huliona cried. "Is this France!?"

"Yes, but…"

"We made it!!" Huliona shouted. "Latopa! Wake up we made it!"

"Wha, what?" Latopa mumbled.

"We made it to France!" Huliona cried.

"We did?"

"Yah!"

Cira watched as the two girls jumped out of the boat and started doing summersaults and cartwheels on the beach. Huliona looked over at the girl.

"Oh, sorry." She said.

"I'm Huliona."

"I'm Latopa."

"Oh hi, I'm Cira."

"I was wondering, what part of France are we in?" Huliona asked.

"You're in Valencia." Cira replied, still baffled.

"Perfect!" Huliona shouted. "Would you mind taking Latopa and I to 43 Mulberry Lane?" Huliona asked.

"If you have a car of course." Latopa said.

"And if it's alright with your parents." Huliona added, nodding towards Cira's parents who were farther down the beach.

"Those are your parent's right?" Latopa asked.

Cira laughed. "Of course!"

All three girls ran down the beach and over to Cira's parents.

"Mom! Dad!" Cira called.

"Yes Cir," Cira's mother started to say, but then she noticed Huliona and Latopa.

"This is Latopa and this is Huliona." Cira said. "They want to know if we can drive them to 43 Mulberry Lane."

"Um, we can certainly drive them," Cira's father said. "but where did they come from?"

"They were in that boat on the beach."

Cira's parents looked confused. "Why were you in the boat?" Cira's mother asked Huliona and Latopa.

"Oh, yah, we still have to tell you that story." Latopa said.

"You can tell us on the way to your, wait where are you going?"

"My uncle's house." Huliona said.

"Yes, on the way to your Uncle's house." Cira's father told them.

So, on the way to Cira's car and on the way to Huliona's uncle's house Huliona and Latopa told Cira and her family everything that happened to them up until when Cira had found them in the dingy.

"That's an amazing story!" Cira said as the car pulled into Huliona's uncle's driveway.

When the car stopped Huliona burst out of the car and started running up the steep driveway. Latopa, Cira, and Cira's family followed close behind.

A girl with blond hair was on the lawn. When she saw Huliona she ran back to the house and yelled something to someone inside.

"Uncle! Huliona has arrived, come quickly."

In a few minutes, Huliona and Rostoa's Uncle was out on the lawn with Rostoa.

Huliona ran to him and flung herself into his arms.

"Good Lord!" Her Uncle shouted. "Huliona, what have you been up too, you're filthy! and I thought there was only one of you." He said as he looked back at Latopa, confused.

"It's a long story Uncle." Huliona said as she looked up at him, tears streaming down her cheeks.

Cira's mother came up to them and said "Mr. Trawson you have a very strong, brave and confident niece."

"Strong? Brave? What have you been up to Huliona?"

"I'll tell you Uncle, but first I must introduce you to my friends. Cira and Latopa."

"Nice to meet you." The girls said.

"Nice to meet you too. Huliona, this is your cousin Rostoa." Huliona's Uncle said as he pointed to the pretty blond girl next to him.

"Nice to meet you at last!" Rostoa said.

Huliona laughed. "Nice to meet you too. Now I need someone to help me tell what I've been up to, or what we've been up to." Huliona motioned for Latopa to come over.

"Everyone, get comfy." Latapa said "It's a long story."

Everyone sat down on the lawn and listened to how Latopa was captured and put on a slave ship and how Huliona had to go to her Uncle's. They were told of the battle when the two boats met up, the fight on the deck of the ship, and how they had gotten away in a dingy. They left out the part about the dolphins.

"That's amazing!" Rostoa said at the end of the tale. "How did you do it?"

"I don't know." Huliona answered "We just did."

"Rosota, why don't you go show Latapa and Huliona to a room." Huliona's uncle said. "I need to talk to Cira's parents. Okay?"

"You can come too Cira." Huliona said.

The four girls ran to the house and up the huge staircase in the entrance hall.

"It's so cool that you're here with me." Huliona told Rostoa as they entered a room with two queen sized beds.

"I know."Answered Rostoa. "I didn't even know you existed until a few days ago!"

"Whoa!" Latopa said, amazed. "These beds are huge!"

"Tell me about it!" Cira said. "My bed is only a twin!"

So, the girls hung out together in Latopa and Huilona's room for a while, talking about all the strange events and odd journeys.

"Cira!" Cira's father called. "It's time to go!"

"But Dad!"

"You'll see the girls tomorrow."

"What?"

"You are going on Mr. Trawson's tour bus to get a look at all the cool sights in France. Then you're going to sleep over."

"He owns a tour company that takes people around France." Rostoa explained.

"Oh." said Cira. "Well see you later guys!"

"Yah, see you tomorrow!" The girls called after Cira as she ran down the stairs.

Chapter 13

THE TOUR

"Mom! What time is the tour? I don't want to miss it!" Clerice called from the hotel bathroom.

"It's in ten minutes!" Clerice's mother answered as she put her silver hoop earrings on.

"Are Christie and Dad coming?" Clerice asked.

"No, they want to check out the gift shops."

Clerice laughed to herself as she put on her strawberry lip gloss, "Gift shops!" Clerice walked out of the bathroom. This was their first day in France; they were taking a tour to learn more about the country.

"Come on!" her mother said as she stood in the doorway. "We don't want to miss the bus."

Clerice grabbed her light blue sweater and hurried out the door after her mother.

When they got outside they saw the tour bus waiting at the bus stop. They hurried down the sidewalk. The bus was scheduled to leave in ten minutes. When they arrived at the bus door Clerice's mother gave the conductor two ten dollar bills.

"Let's sit on the top row!" Clerice said.

"Alright." Clerice's mother said.

They both climbed to the top level of the bus. Clerice sat in front of and open window, she loved to watch the sky zoom by when she was in the car. A minute later another girl her age came and sat down with her brothers and parents, it was a tight squeeze Clerice and the other girl were hip to hip.

"Oh, sorry!" the girl said as she accidentally bumped Clerice's elbow.

"Oh, no it's okay." Clerice said.

"I love to sit on the top." The other girl said. "It's closest to the sun."

Clerice laughed. "Me too, I like to watch the sky."

"Other people think I'm weird for saying that!" the other girl said.

"Yah, lots of people think I'm strange for loving the sky so much." Clerice said.

"Oh, by the way I'm Cira."

****

"Hurry up Latopa!" Rostoa called from the hallway.

"Yes, hurry!" Huliona added. "The bus leaves in a few minutes."

Suddenly the bedroom door was flung wide and Latopa was standing there.

"I'm sorry." She said. "I was just thinking about my family. I really hope they are okay." Latopa closed the door and followed Huliona and Rostoa down the stairs.

"We're going to get them back Latopa." Huliona said.

"Yes, we promise." Rostoa added.

"Now let's go girls we don't want to keep Cira waiting." Huliona said.

"Girls where are you?" Huliona and Rostoa's Uncle called from downstairs.

"We're coming Uncle!" Rostoa answered as the three girls ran the rest of the way down the long flight of stairs.

Once they reached the bottom, Huliona, Latopa, Rostoa and Mr. Trawson hurried out of the house and down the driveway. They ran down the street and turned a corner and came to the big white tour bus. The girls saw Cira waving from the top level.

"Hey guys!" she called. "I made us a new friend!"

"Hey Cira!" Latopa called back.

The girls and Huliona and Rostoa's Uncle boarded the bus. Huliona, Latopa and Rostoa climbed to the top level. They searched for Cira; she was near the back of the bus.

"Hey." Huliona said as she sat next to Cira.

"What's up?" Rostoa said.

"So who's our new friend?" Latopa asked, sitting down.

"Rostoa, Huliona, Latopa, this is Clerice." Cira motioned to a pretty girl with brown hair and blue eyes.

"Nice to meet you." Clerice said.

"Nice to meet you too." The others exclaimed.

"I heard your story, that's amazing!" Clerice said.

The girls got to talking as the bus started to move. They laughed and told jokes like they were old friends. But suddenly the bus screeched to a stop.

The five girls ran to the front window to see what was happening. As they looked out of the front of the bus they saw they had almost run over two girls, in fluffy winter coats.

Chapter 14

MIRROR

"Eliana!" Hatara called. "Are you alright?"

The two girls were in the middle of the street on the ground. They had almost been run over by a huge bus.

"Are we dead?" Eliana asked.

"No, the bus stopped in time. Thank heavens!" Hatara answered.

The girls looked up. They saw five girls running toward them, concerned looks on all their faces.

"Oh my gosh! Are you okay?" one of them asked.

"Umm, yes we're okay." Hatara said.

"Who are you?" another asked. "And what were you doing in the middle of the road?"

"I'm Hatara."

"And I'm Eliana."

"Nice to meet you. I'm Rostoa. This is Huliona, Cira, Clerice, and Latopa."

"Hi."

"Nice to meet you."

"Hello."

"Hey." The other girls said.

In that second the wind picked up, the clouds turned gray and the loudest clap of thunder the girls had ever heard sounded. It seemed to say "SEVEN!". Then it started to pour down rain.

Everyone was drenched immediately.

"What in the world!?" the girls heard Mr. Trawson say. "It wasn't supposed to rain today!"

"Clerice!" Clerice looked up and saw her mother running towards her with a suitcase. "I've been talking to Mr. Trawson; it turns out we went to college together we are old friends. The other girls are sleeping over his house, would you like to join them?"

"Awsome!!" Clerice said, excited. She took her suitcase.

"Hey!" Huliona and Rostoa's Uncle yelled as he ran over. "Are you girls okay?"

"Yes, we're fine sir!" Eliana answered.

Huliona and Rostoa's uncle walked over to them.

"I'm Mr. Trawson." He said. "Huliona and Rostoa's Uncle."

"Nice to meet you." Hatara said.

"And you." Mr. Trawson said. "But where are your parents?" he asked.

"My parents are dead." Eliana answered.

"And mine are in Greenland." Hatara added.

"In Greenland but, what, how did you get here?" Mr. Trawson asked, now utterly confused.

"We got attacked by a leopard seal, ended up stuck on an ice block, drifted a ways," Eliana looked over at Hatara. "Then a ship picked us up and dropped us off here."

Mr. Trawson narrowed his eyes, suspiciously.

"Oh, you don't believe us?" Hatara said meekly.

"Are you kidding?!" Cira said. "Of course we believe you!"

"Hu?" Eliana and Hatara said together.

"We've been through some pretty strange stuff ourselves." Huliona said, taking a quick glance at her ring.

"Well, anyway." Mr. Trawson said. "Does anyone know you're here?"

"No." Eliana answered.

"Oh! You should come back to the house with us!" Clerice said.

"Yes, you can get some warm clothes and we'll find a way to get you home." Latopa said.

Eliana and Hatara looked at the girls in amazement.

"You would do that for us?" Hatara asked.

"Of Course!" Huliona said. "Trust me; we know what you've been through."

"Well, if you insist." Eliana said.

Cira and Rostoa helped Hatara and Eliana up, then the eight of them hurried down the cobbled street towards the house.

****

"Would you girls like some more tea?" Jostle the maid asked Eliana and Hatara.

"Yes please." Eliana replied, finishing what was in her cup.

"So a seal attacked you?" Latopa said, sticking her feet out in front of the warm fire. She took another sip of tea.

"Yes." Hatara said. "It was a big one too! It was really scary!"

"I'm not trying to sound mean," Clerice said. "but that is so cool!"

"Yeah, I guess it was." Eliana agreed with a laugh.

"Well your story sounded pretty amazing too!" Hatara said. "Being put on a slave ship, and then your boats meeting up, it was a miracle!"

"I know." said Huliona. "Just think of what would have happened to Latopa."

"I don't like too." Latopa said.

"Uncle?" Rostoa asked. "Can we all sleep in the library tonight?"

"That's a fantastic idea!" Cira exclaimed.

"Yes it is uncle!"

"Please!"

"Oh yes let us sleep there!"

"Well if you really want to."

A cheer rose up among the girls. About an hour later all of them had brushed their teeth and gotten into their pajamas, they were heading for the library.

"I love your kitty pajamas!" Clerice said to Latopa.

Latopa laughed. "I found them in an old trunk Huliona said I'd find clothes in." She did a twirl. "I am quite fond of your polka-dots!"

"Why thank you!" Clerice said laughing.

The seven girls entered the library. Rostoa closed the oak doors behind them. Once they were all settled they walked over to a half circle window seat and sat down to talk.

"Um, guys?" Huliona said."There is something Latopa and I left out of our story."

"Yeah," Latopa said. "and I think we should tell you."

"What is it?" Rostoa asked.

"Well, when I was on the slave ship something very strange happened to me," Latopa said.

The girls were silent, and a little worried.

"Well I looked over the side of the boat to watch the waves because I was sad. I saw a dolphin, so I said hi to it, but then, it said hi back."

Everyone was silent, staring at Latopa wide eyed.

"But that's not all," Huliona said. "When we were escaping into the dingy, and that man we told you about grabbed us, the sea sprayed up onto the deck, bringing with it pieces of sea grass." Huliona gulped. "When I picked up the sea grass I felt a surge of power run through me, then it formed into this." Huliona held up the ring.

Everyone gasped.

"But, but, how?" Cira stuttered.

"I don't know." Huliona said. "It was the strangest thing."

"And when we got into the dingy," Latopa said. "The dolphin I talked to and its friend helped us get away."

"Um, we also have something to tell you guys." Eliana said. "We weren't sure if we could trust you at first. But now we know we can."

"Yes," said Hatara. "But never tell anyone what we are going to say."

"Our lips are sealed." Clerice said.

So, Eliana and Hatara told the five other girls about how Hatara had blown them miles across the ocean and how when Eliana had pulled her hand out of the water the water droplets formed the four words, LOOK TO THE RIGHT.

"That's, that's amazing!" Latopa said.

"There's more." Rostoa said.

"Spill!" Huliona said.

"Okay you guys ready?"

"Yeah."

"Go ahead."

"Okay." Rostoa started. "Well, a couple of days before Huliona and Latopa arrived I was outside looking for things to make Huliona a gift with. Then I heard a voice. I turned around but no one was there. Then I heard it again, it said 'Etarfia was in danger tell the others.'"

The moment Rostoa said Etarfia all the girls got a far away look in their eyes, as if remembering something that happened long ago.

Huliona muttered it under her breath, "Etarfia."

After she muttered it everyone snapped back to life.

"I didn't know who the others were, but the voice said I will know them when I see them. And I think, the others, are you guys."

****

The girls lay on a giant blow up mattress in front of a mirror on the far right side of the library.

"So you think we're these mystical others?" Huliona asked.

"Yes." Rostoa said. "The voice said you will know them when you see them."

"Well we don't even know what or where Etarfia is!" Latopa exclaimed, irritated.

"It could have been a prank." Eliana suggested.

"Yeah, just a couple of kids." Hatara said.

"It wasn't a prank! I swear!"

"Did the voice give any clues to where Etarfia might be?" Clerice asked.

"No. Not one!"

"Have you told your uncle?" Cira asked.

"No way! He would think I'm a psycho path!" Rostoa answered.

"Well what are we supposed to do?" Eliana asked. "Sit and wait?"

"No we're not going to wait, we're going to find this Etarfia and save it from any danger it is in!" Huliona declared.

"Well if we're going to find Etarfia we need to get some rest." Hatara said.

"You're right." Clerice agreed.

So all the girls curled up under the fluffy down quilt on the large blow up mattress. They soon fell asleep, oblivious to what would happen next.

****

Dong, dong, dong, the clock sounded. Huliona woke with a start. She glanced at the clock, midnight.

"Stupid clock." She muttered, half asleep.

Huliona sat up and looked around. There was something very eerie about the library. Something just didn't feel right.

"Strange, there's no moon." She exclaimed as she stole a look out the window. She then looked at her new friends, "Guess I was the only one woken up. Might as well get a glass of water."

Huliona stood up, ready to pick her way around everyone but before she took one step a flash of green light blinded her.

"Ahh!"

As the light dimmed she saw it was coming from her ring.

"What the…"

Then out of the corner of her eye she saw something was happening to the mirror. Huliona looked over and reeled back in horror, sparkles of every color were whirling around the mirror. A shape was forming in the mirror as well, and it wasn't her own.

"Guys! GUYS!" Huliona screamed.

"Wha, what, what!" everyone started to say, and then they saw what was happening to the mirror.

The six on the mattress scrambled over to Huliona. Then all seven of them clutched each other with fear and confusion, and curiosity in their eyes.

"What's happening!?" Rostoa shouted over the noise.

"I'll tell you what's happening!" Cira yelled. "We've found your mysterious voice!"

Chapter 15

SAFFERSTAR

The sparkles had settled, the glow from the ring had dimmed, and the noise had stopped. The only remaining thing from the strange event that had just occurred was the surprised look on the girls' faces.

A small thin creature stood before the seven girls on the mattress. It looked like an elf only it was taller and had narrow face features. On its backs it had very small, shredded, light green wings.

She gave the girls a smile and said. "So, we finally meet at last girls. I have waited 97 years for you."

All the girls especially Huliona were shaking uncontrollably.

"Who are you?" Clerice squeaked.

"I'm Safferstar, a sprite kin. You are Clerice. The others are Hatara, Huliona, Eliana, Rostoa, Cira, and Latopa. Why are you looking at me so strangely? Have you not seen a sprite before?"

"No we have not seen a sprite before!" Latopa said bravely.

"Are you the voice I heard?" Rostoa asked.

"I am."

"Then what's Etarfia? And why are you here?"

"Your first question, Etarfia is a magical land formed many many years ago. Your second question, I have always been here."

"Always?" Hatara asked.

"Yes, I am you girls' guardian."

"Guardian?!" Eliana said, disbelievingly. "There is no such thing!"

"Who do you think kept you alive on that ice block?! Who do you think helped Huliona and Latopa's boat drift to the very beach Cira was at after the dolphins left?!"

"So it's true." Cira said.

"Of course it's true!" Safferstar said, she turned her back on the girls, her green earth toned dress swinging around her knees.

"I'm sorry." Eliana said.

"It's alright." Safferstar said. "I know this is a big surprise for you all."

"So what do you want?" Huliona asked, stepping forward.

"You must come save Etarfia of course!" Safferstar said, nearly falling over from excitement.

"What? Save Etarfia?" Clerice said.

"Yes! Rostoa got my message, did she not?"

"Well yes, but…what can we do?" Huliona asked.

"What can you do!? What can you do!? You can do a lot! You can save a whole realm!" Safferstar was beaming. "You are the Queens of Etarfia!"

"QUEENS!!!!!" Rostoa cried.

"YES!" Safferstar answered.

"OMG COOL!!!" Clerice said, jumping up and down with excitement.

"You all have special powers too."

"Like what?" Latopa asked.

"I'll tell you on the way too Etarfia." Safferstar said.

Safferstar then walked over to the mirror, preparing to step inside.

"Coming?" she asked.

"Can you give us a minute?" Huliona asked.

"Sure."

The girls huddled together.

"Guys, I'm not so sure about this." Huliona whispered.

"Why? What's the matter?" Hatara asked.

"Well for one thing, this all seems too good to be true. For another, can we trust her?"

"Huliona!" Clerice said. "When is the last time you've seen a real sprite kin?"

"Never." Huliona said.

"Well then how do you know we can't trust a sprite kin?"

"Yah," Eliana said. "Give her a chance."

"I think Huliona has something here." Cira said. "I mean this is all really strange. A magical land? Is this for real?"

"Cira!" Latopa said a little too loud. "There is a REAL sprite kin in the library with us!"

Rostoa looked over at Safferstar to see her staring at them looking worried.

So, after a few more minutes of arguing, the girls came out of their huddle and Huliona said."Yes, we're coming."

Chapter 16

STORIES

"So we have to go through the mirror?" Clerice said.

"Yes." Safferstar said.

"Will it hurt?" Cira asked, eyeing the mirror with doubt.

Safferstar laughed. "Of course not!"

"Why did you come in through the mirror?" Huliona asked. "Cant you just fly here?"

"Yah," Eliana said. "Like in *Never land*."

"Haha! Those are just old wise tales!" Safferstar said. "Magical creatures can only come to the human world through mirrors. We have to come at exactly midnight too."

"Oh." Latopa said.

Rostoa touched her finger to the mirror, it sank through. She quickly pulled it back. "It's cold!" She exclaimed.

"Oh come on! We don't have all night!" Safferstar said.

"Okay you guys ready?" Hatara asked.

"Ready as we'll ever be." The others answered.

Safferstar went first, followed by Hatara, Eliana, Cira, Rostoa, Huliona, Clerice and finally Latopa. When the last girl stepped out of the mirror all Etarfia seemed to shudder.

"They know." Safferstar said.

"Who know what?" Rostoa asked.

"They know you girls are here."

The girls looked around them; they were in a dark forest shrouded in a thick fog.

"Who knows?" Eliana asked.

"You're people for goodness sake!"

"Our people?"

"Oh sorry, you're subjects." Safferstar said. "There's the path!" she announced as she ran into the fog.

"Wait!" the girls shouted as they ran after her.

They finally caught up with Safferstar.

"This place is creepy." Latopa exclaimed as they continued deeper into the forest.

"So what's the story of Etarfia?" Huliona asked, changing the subject.

"Oh I was hoping you'd ask!" Safferstar said happily.

****

"It all began long ago when Etarfia was a regular country. It was a part of Europe, a wonderful vacation spot. I was young, fifteen or so,"

"You were a human?!" Huliona exclaimed.

"Yes, now don't interrupt!" Safferstar said.

"Sorry!" Huliona said.

"As I said I was fifteen or so when strange men came to the island. They were searching for something, but wouldn't tell anyone what they were looking for. They also brought eight girls with them. But one of the girls was set apart. She was quiet, solitary and kept to her self most of the time. She was very beautiful. I ended up befriending her. She was very different from others who were vain and mean, always snapping at anyone in their path, then whispering together. Everyone on the island was superstitious. They thought there was something special about these strange people, especially, my new friend. As it turned out, there was. My new friend had a necklace with seven gems on it. One was dark green the others sparkling clear, ocean blue, another deep brown, a stormy grey, a warm yellow and a berry crimson. Then one day I mentioned how beautiful it was. She then told me that she had a secret to tell me. We went far into the woods and as we walked she told me that the girls that had come with her were really witches from another realm, and they had come to take over the island. She told me she was a witch as well, but did not agree with what the others were trying to do, so she wanted to help. I was Shocked, and I asked her what we should do. She said the only way to beat magic, was with magic. My new friend said that if it ever came to the witches trying to take over the island then I should take her necklace into the woods and smash it on top of the biggest rock I could find. She did not go into detail about what would happen, but she said that something magical would happen that would help everyone on the island defeat the witches. She also said that along with the magical occurrence, seven special girls, girls who were different from all the rest would be chosen from earth to become best friends and the Queens of the island, now called Etarfia, would come to help us save it from the witches with their powers represented by each of the gems."

By now all the girls were silent. Awestruck, and almost all their mouths were hanging open. The story continued.

"One day, she became very ill. I called the doctor to come and see her. After he looked her over, he told me she was going to die. He said she had a rare type of cancer that could not be cured. A few days later I went to visit her. It was a gloomy day, perfect for the circumstances. But when I went to her room, she had a glassy look in her eyes, she was clutching her necklace and muttering to herself. When she saw me she motioned for me to come over. When I came over she took my hand and said the time had come, the witches were planning to take over the island that vary night. She gave me her necklace and closed my hand over it. She said 'smash it, smash it, you mustn't let the witches win'. I nodded, and just as she finished her head dropped to her chest. The cancer had won. I ran from the room, tears blurring my vision, but I had a mission. I ran into the woods and found a large rock. I put the necklace on the rock, took a smaller one ready to smash it. Just as I was going to smash the necklace I heard a voice behind me. I turned; one of the seven other girls was behind me. She told me to give her the necklace that it was important. I looked into her eyes hoping my friend had been wrong, but her eyes did not look right. I screamed 'liar!' She was enraged then rushed for me, but before she reached me I brought my rock down and smashed the necklace. Then everything went black. When I awoke, it seemed hours later, I immediately knew something was wrong. I stood but when I did I seemed shorter. I ran to a puddle near by and looked down. I was indeed much shorter, so was my hair, I even had wings! I almost fainted at my reflection, but I knew I had to go see if everyone else was okay."

"I ran through the island, I saw people like me, people that had turned into balls of light and air, there were rock giants and mushroom people, fairies, and pixies. Others had been turned into mertoids, dirt people, and cloud people. I saw talking animals and plant horses and all other sorts of creatures. I knew then, that my life had change forever."

"So that's how Etarfia started." Eliana exclaimed.

"Yes." Safferstar answered.

"Hey, where did the seven witches go?" Cira asked.

Safferstar stopped in her tracks and looked at Cira darkly.

"That's why you're here." She said.

"What?" Latopa asked.

"When I awoke they were gone, but awhile later they came back. The necklace had enhanced their powers. They had also found a way to expand their life span. And the same day I smashed the necklace you girls were chosen as the queens of Etarfia."

"But we weren't even born yet." Clerice said.

"That didn't matter." Safferstar said. "The necklace chose you."

"So you said the witches came back?" Huliona said.

"Yes, they are still here, and they are on their way to taking over Etarfia. You girls are here to stop that."

"How are we going to do that!?" Rostoa asked. "We don't know anything about fighting!"

Safferstar reached into the only pocket on her dress and pulled out six gems.

"The gems from the story!" the girls exclaimed.

"I better start with your powers." Safferstar said, kneeling down on one knee. "Hatara step forward." Hatara did so. "Queen Hatara you have the power of wind and air." Safferstar placed the clear gem in Hatara's hand. "Rostoa step forward. Queen Rostoa you have the power of stone and earth." Safferstar placed the brown gem in Rostoa's hand. "Latopa step forward. Queen Latopa you have the power of all animals." Safferstar placed the crimson gem in Latopa's hand. "Cira step forward. Queen Cira you have the power of fire, magma, and light." Safferstar placed the yellow gem in Cira's hand. "Clerice step forward. Queen Clerice you have the power of weather." Safferstar placed the grey gem in Clerice's hand. "Eliana step

forward. Queen Eliana you have the power of water and ice."
Safferstar placed the blue gem in Eliana's hand. There was only
Huliona left.

"Do I not have a power?" Huliona squeaked, looking sad.

"Oh, Huliona of course!" Safferstar said. "You have your
gem already."

Huliona looked down at her ring. "Is this it?" she asked,
holding it up.

"It is."

"Well, why did I get my gem before everyone else?"

"Ummm, well…" Safferstar said looking guilty. "The day
after Etarfia came into being, I, I, dropped one of the gems in
the sea as I was flying over it. It was yours Huliona. I'm sorry. I
looked for years, but I couldn't find it. A few days ago the gem
must have sensed that the day when you girls were to come to
Etarfia was near, so it found you."

"Found me?" Huliona said in amazement.

Safferstar nodded.

"Oh. What's my power?" Huliona asked.

"Queen Huliona," Safferstar said kneeling. "Your power is
plants and fungus."

Suddenly Hatara cried out, "Look!"

Everyone looked towards Hatara in amazement; a white
staff with her gem on top was forming in Hatara's hand.

"It's beautiful!" The girls exclaimed.

"Guys!" Rostoa cried out.

The girls looked over at Rostoa. She was holding a crown. It
was a thin band of silver with her gem set into the center.

"Mine just turned into a bracelet!" Eliana exclaimed.

"Oh! Mine just turned into a necklace!" Latopa cried out.

"OOO!! A broach!" Clerice said.

"Mine turned into and armband!" Cira said.

Everyone looked over at Huliona.

"Mine had already turned into a ring." Huliona said shrugging.

The girls put their gems on.

"We need to get moving."Safferstar said, as she ran down the path.

But as the girls ran after her, no one noticed the wings forming on Hatara's back.

Chapter 17

MISSING

"Mr. Trawson! Their gone! Their gone!" Jostle the maid called as she burst through Mr. Trawsons bedroom door.

"Wha, what!" Mr. Trawson called sitting bolt upright.

"The girls, their gone!" Jostle wheezed, out of breath.

"WHAT!!!" Mr. Trawson roared. "Their GONE!!"

Jostle nodded. Mr. Trawson jumped out of bed and ran to the library. He burst in calling all their names. None of them answered. He ran over to the big empty mattress. There were different colored sparkles every where.

"Jostle!" Mr. Trawson called.

"Yes Mr. Trawson?"

"Check all the rooms!"

"I did."

"Well check again!"

Jostle ran through the house checking all the rooms and calling for the girls. Meanwhile Mr. Trawson called the police.

"Jostle I'm checking outside. The police are on their way."

"Alright Mr. Trawson!" Jostle answered.

Mr. Trawson was checking outside when the police arrived. The chief approached Mr. Trawson.

"Sir, please state your issue again for my men."

"Both my niece's and their friends are gone!"

"How many girls were there all together?" the chief asked.

"Seven." Mr. Trawson answered.

"Alright, men, fan out! Check everywhere. And sir, I'll need to ask you a few questions."

"Yes, yes of course." Mr. Trawson answered.

But the police did not know, the worried uncle, did not know, no one knew that they would not find the girls.

Chapter 18

KATRINA

The girls hurried through the dark forest, looking about them all the time. Cira was very afraid. She kept thinking she saw creatures moving in the shadows, and she didn't know where she was going.

"Ahh!" Huliona screamed.

"Huliona!!" the girls shouted.

"Where are you?!" Eliana called.

"I'm over here!"

When the girls found Huliona, Safferstar started to laugh.

"It's not funny!" Huliona shouted.

The girls started to laugh too. Huliona was hanging from a vine upside-down.

"This vine just reached out and grabbed my ankle!" Huliona said. "Then it pulled me up!"

"The vine is only greeting its Queen!" Safferstar laughed.

"Greeting me?" Huliona asked.

"Yes."

"Oh."

The girls laughed even harder.

"Guys!" Huliona cried out in surprise. "The vine is talking to me!"

"Talking to you?" Clerice asked in surprise.

"Yes, it says danger is about my Queen, it also says," Huliona said, listening hard. "it's heading right for us!!"

Once Hulionoa said this, vines shot down from the trees and picked up all the girls, except for Hatara and Safferstar. Safferstar flapped her little wings and flew up to where the others were hanging.

"What about me!?" Hatara screamed franticly.

"Fly!" Safferstar yelled.

"I don't have wings! I can't fly!" Hatara whined.

"Hatara! You do have wings! Look!" Latopa cried out in surprise.

Hatara looked behind her, a pair of beautiful milky white wings sat perfectly on her back.

"I don't know how to move them!" Hatara sobbed.

Suddenly the wind picked up and whispered to Hatara, "We will help you."

The wind blew really hard and lifted her into the air. Hatara tried to flap her wings as hard as she could, and when the wind died down she found that she was still in the air. Hatara flew up to the others. Just as she reached them the girls heard someone or something crashing through the forest.

Whatever it was crashed into the clearing the girls had been standing in only minutes before. The creature looked around and sniffed the air. The girls looked at it wide eyed. It was like a huge wolf, only its fur looked rough and spiky and its tail was only a stub.

"Come out come out wherever you are!" the creature growled mockingly. "I know you're here my *Queens*! Your scent is strong!"

"Wha, what is it?" Eliana stuttered quietly.

"It's a sabberon." Safferstar answered.

"What's a sabberon?" Rostoa whispered.

"It's a half wolf half cat-like creature, very evil beings."

"Ahh, there you are!" the sabberon hissed.

The girls looked down in horror; the sabberon was smiling up at them wickedly, displaying a row of razor sharp teeth.

"Leave us alone!" Cira yelled bravely.

The sabberon laughed like it was the funniest thing he had ever heard. "I'm sorry my dear, I cannot do that…you see I work for the dark majesties and they have ordered me to kill you."

"Kill us?" Cira squeaked, suddenly not feeling so brave.

The sabberon smiled. "Now if you'll excuse me, I must obey their request." Just as the sabberon was about to lunge for the girl's a horn sounded, loud and clear.

Suddenly darting balls of light surrounded the clearing, dimming to reveal starfs, or light people. Clunes or cloud people materialized next to them. Mushroom men jumped down from the trees, mertoids rose up from the river near by and stepped out of the water, their clothes flowing behind them as if they were still under the waves, their legs covered in scales. Dirt rose up from the ground in forms of people. Animals streamed out of dark corners and sprites and fairies flew into view. They were all armed.

"You're surrounded." A voice said. A tall girl with curly blond shoulder length hair stepped into the clearing. She pulled a sword from her belt.

"Katrina!" Safferstar said in relief.

"My Queens! Katrina shouted up to them. I am Katrina, your trainer and army captain. I have come to save you!"

The sabberon laughed. "You will be doing no saving today."

"If you want to live," Katrina said in a dangerously low voice. "You will not harm the Queens, now get out!"

The sabberon looked around him, seeing how surrounded he was, then seemed to reconsider.

"Oh I'm leaving," He said. "But I'll be back to silence those blasted Queen's once and for all!"

"You have decided your fate!" Katrina roared, rushing at the sabberon with her sword.

"No!" Latopa yelled. She pounded on the vine that held her, it let go of her waist and Latopa fell to the ground.

Just before Katrina reached the sabberon Latopa jumped in front of him.

****

Katrina stopped short. "My Queen! What are you doing? Out of the way, he will kill you!"

Latopa turned to the sabberon, he looked stunned and afraid, and Latopa knelt down and peered into his eyes. The whole clearing seemed to be holding its breath.

"You were not always evil, were you?" Latopa finally said.

This enraged the sabberon. "I am evil now! Being evil is my true nature! Being good is for the weak!"

"But being evil is ruining Etarfia, you can be good again, and help us save it." Latopa said.

"NEVER!!" the sabberon suddenly lunged for Latopa.

Terrified Latopa turned and ran from the clearing and into a larger one, with the sabberon at her heels. With the wolves and deer in the lead all the animals in the clearing tore after the sabberon and their Queen.

Latopa's heart was pounding; she could hear her blood rushing in her ears. Then, suddenly she wasn't in Etarfia; she was back in Egypt running from the pirates who had taken her and her family. She was almost to the Nile. Latopa tripped and fell onto the soft grass before her, she was back in Etarfia. She whirled around the sabberon was on her! But before the sabberon could lunge a mighty deer butted the sabberon in the side, sending him flying.

The sabberon landed near by with a painful thud. Wolves and foxes circled him snarling and baring their teeth.

"Get out!" a huge grey and black wolf snarled. The foxes snapped at the sabberons back legs. The sabberon turned and fled into the wood. A cheer rose up among the animals. The deer rose up on their hind legs and bellowed triumphantly.

Latopa felt dizzy. She heard muffled cries that seemed far away. 'Latopa!' they seemed to say. She looked up, her friends were running towards her, and then everything went black.

****

Latopa opened her eyes. Light surrounded her. She looked around. At first Latopa thought she was in a stone box, but then her eyes came into focus and she saw she was in a large courtyard. It was made of a pinkish stone, and it had trees in all four corners. Huliona was in one corner leaning against one of the trees muttering to her self. Clerice was crying not far off with Eliana trying to comfort her. Katrina was sharpening her sword. Hatara and Cira were talking in low tones in the back left corner and Rostoa was fighting with Safferstar.

"No one likes it here!" Rostoa shouted. "Clerice is having a mental break down, Huliona is going nuts! And Latopa was almost killed!"

Safferstar looked at her toes. "I thought you knew." She said.

"Knew what?"

"That this was not going to be safe and easy." Safferstar answered.

"Well I didn't know that we would almost be killed every five seconds! I don't think the girls and I can take this, so we will be leaving in the morning." Rostoa said.

"What!? You can't go! All Etarfia will be lost!"

"We're leaving and that's,"

Huliona had just walked over with Latopa trailing behind followed by Cira, Hatara, Eliana, and the sobbing Clerice.

"What are you talking about?" Huliona asked.

"We're leaving Huliona." Rostoa told her.

"No we can't go!"

"Huliona, Latopa was almost killed and we'll be next if we don't get out of here!"

"But we can't just leave our people to die!"

"I think *our* people can fend for themselves! Look at the way they saved Latopa!"

As the girls argued Clerice became not as much sad but angry. And as her anger boiled up inside her the clouds turned grey and the sky rumbled, threatening a storm. When the girls still did not stop arguing Clerice threw up her hands and lightning shot out of them and streaked across the sky.

"Stop!" she roared.

Rostoa and Huliona shut their mouths and pulled back, now a bit frightened.

"This arguing is not helping anyone!" Clerice raged.

"I'm trying to make Huliona see sense! What else am I supposed to do?" Rostoa said.

"Stay and fight." Cira said stepping forward.

"We'll get killed!" Rostoa said.

"But it's the right thing to do!" Huliona shot back.

"Shut up Huliona!" Rostoa shouted.

"Okay," Hatara said nervously. "Calm down."

"Oh! I'm so sorry! You wouldn't know the right thing to do if it hit you in the face!" Huliona shouted.

"What!? Didn't your stupid mother teach you to stay out of danger? Don't play in the street Huliona!" Rostoa taunted.

The fight was now out of control.

Huliona lunged for Rostoa shouting, "At least I had a mother!"

Rostoa jumped aside and Huliona hit the ground with a thud. Then without knowing what they were doing, the two girls activated their gems.

Chapter 19

THE FIGHT

Rostoa's gem flared. She thrust her hands towards the ground. She turned them in weird directions. Then suddenly a huge chunk of rock lifted from the ground. Rostoa steadied it in the air, and then thrust her hands towards Huliona sending the rock flying towards her cousin.

Huliona put her hand in front of her face. She whispered something to her ring then it glowed fiercely. A green shield surrounded Huliona. The rock hit the shield full force dissolving on impact sending sparks flying everywhere.

Huliona threw herself into the air. Vines shot from her hands rapping around Rostoa, squeezing her hard.

Rostoa looked at some small sharp rocks nearby, she nodded to them. The rocks shot up and through the air slicing the vines, freeing Rostoa.

Just as the girls were about to strike out at each other again Latopa yelled, "It's time to kick some butt!" she raced towards Huliona and Rostoa. But as Latopa ran she turned into a mighty mountain lion. She jumped on Rostoa pinning her to the ground.

Eliana had followed close behind. She shot water out of her hands, surrounding Huliona in a water bubble.

"Now that's enough!" Latopa roared, literally.

Rostoa squirmed and Huliona banged on the water bubble. Latopa got off Rostoa and turned back into herself and Eliana released the water bubble, Huliona was soaking wet. Hatara walked over to Huliona and blasted her with a strong wind, drying her off. Safferstar and Katrina looked furious.

"What in all Etarfia were you thinking!?" Katrina yelled. "I have not trained you!"

"That was very foolish!" Safferstar said. "You could have hurt each other!"

Both girls looked down. "The only thing foolish here is Huliona." Rostoa said.

Huliona shot Rostoa the nastiest look any of the girls had ever seen, then, she turned and ran.

Chapter 20

THE MISTING MEMORY POOL

"I'll follow her." Hatara said. She lifted into the air and flew off after her friend.

Huliona ran from the courtyard and into a long dark hallway, she heard Hatara calling her name but she ignored her. Huliona ran faster past the crumbling walls and decaying rafters. She entered a forest. It was not like the forest she and the girls had just been in, but pitch black except for a small faintly glowing blue light up ahead.

Hatara flew up beside her. "Huliona, are you okay?" she asked.

"No!"

"We need to move on and get over this."

"I can't! How can Rostoa just leave these people? Our people?"

"Well if it makes you feel any better, I'm staying."

Huliona gave a weak smile. Just as Hatara was about to say something more a blue sparkling light shot past them. The light circled them then landed on a bush near their feet. As the light dimmed it revealed a fairy perching on the very end of a long branch of the bush. The fairy looked at them and smiled.

"My! Oh wonderful Queen Hatara, it is an honor to be in your presence!" She said. "As well as you Queen Huliona." The fairy bowed deeply. She was completely blue except for her wings hair and dress. Her wings were a milky white, similar to Hatara's. Her dress was made out of white cobwebs that reached her knees, and she had curly dark brown hair that was pulled back into a bun with flowers as the elastic. "I am Moyan, a moonbeam fairy."

The two girls were fascinated as they stared at the small creature. "Um, hello Moyan." Hatara said glancing over at Huliona.

"Are you lost my Queens?" Moyan asked.

"No, at least, I don't think so." Huliona answered. She looked past Moyan and said "Are those more of your people?" Huliona nodded towards the blue light.

Moyan looked at the two girls darkly. "No," she said. "that is a Misting Memory Pool. One of the many things in Etarfia you should stay away from."

"Why?" Hatara asked. "What does it do?"

"My people say that if you look into a Misting Memory pool it will show you the things that were important to you. Then when you are caught off guard, or when you are leaning over the water far enough, it will suck you into its dark waters."

"Wow." Huliona said.

"It is a creation of the dark witches." Moyan added. "There is also said to be a secret hidden in the pools, but no one is brave enough to look for it."

"How can you hide a secret?" Hatara asked.

"This is a magical world Queen Hatara! Almost anything is possible!" Moyan said with a smile.

Hatara laughed. "Yes I suppose your right!"

"Guys, I feel kind of weird, I'm feeling a strange energy." Huliona said.

"Me too." Hatara agreed.

"Yes, let's go." Moyan said. "But I do wish I found those ree-grass berries I was looking for! Going through here is the quickest way to get to them."

The girls laughed, and just as they turned to leave trees and thorn bushes moved in front of them blocking their path. They stumbled back in fear. Then they heard a rustling behind them, they turned. The trees were moving aside, forming a path, leading strait to the misting memory pool.

Moyan looked alarmed. "We need to leave!" she said. "Now!" But as she said this a whisper was heard.

"Queens, Queens of Etarfia, come to me and I will show you your desires." The whisper was coming from the pool.

"Don't listen!" Moyan shouted, now terrified. But it was too late, Huliona and Hatara, out of curiosity, were heading strait for the Misting Memory Pool.

Chapter 21

MIRACLE

After Huliona and Hatara had gone Safferstar and Katrina had gone into a corner and started to talk in low tones. While they did this, all the other girls activated their gems. They fiddled with their powers for a while; Clerice accidentally made it rain, snow, sleet, and hail all at the same time, then they all decided to set up camp using their powers. All of them were exhausted and needed some sleep.

Eliana made an igloo that amazingly didn't melt even in Etarfia's warm air. Rostoa picked up some rocks and piled them into a cave. Clerice made a small tornado, turned it upside down then carved out a door. Cira made a real giant sunflower, literally. And Latopa turned into a fox and dug a den. It was very quiet throughout the courtyard, even Safferstar and Katrina had fallen asleep. But Cira and Clerice found it hard to sleep, so they stayed up and talked.

"Hey," Cira said. "Huliona and Hatara have been gone a long time."

"Yeah, they have." agreed Clerice. "A little over a half an hour."

Cira leaned in close to Clerice and whispered this time "That was some fight."

"I know." Clerice answered. "I thought they were going to kill each other."

Cira looked sad. "I hope Huliona is okay."

"Me too." Clerice said. "Do you want to go look for her and Hatara? You know just to make sure everything is alright?'

"Yes, let's go." Cira said.

But just as the two girls stood to leave a blue light came zooming toward them. It hit Cira in the stomach, knocking her over.

"Oh! My Queen I am so sorry!" the blue light said. As the blue light dimmed the girls saw it was not a light at all, it was a fairy, with dark hair, milky white wings, and a cobweb dress.

****

"I am Moyan, a Moonbeam fairy. I have come to tell you that your fellow Queen's Queen Huliona and Queen Hatara are in great danger!"

"What!" Clerice yelled.

"Yes, I was flying through the Gable Night Forest when I came upon them. We had a nice chat but when we tried to leave, the forest would not let us. It then formed a path leading strait to a Misting Memory Pool!"

"What's a Misting Memory Pool?" Cira asked.

"Misting Memory Pools are usually in dark places. They entice you into coming over to them. Then when you are looking into its dark waters it mists over and shows you the things that were important to you. So when you are leaning over far enough it, it…" Moyan burst into tears.

Cira glanced over at Clerice. "Just take us to the forest." Clerice said. "Everything will be fine."

But Clerice wasn't sure everything would be fine, if what she thought Moyan was trying to tell them had happened.

Chapter 22

TAILS

Eliana woke with a start. She had been dreaming about her family when she had heard a loud crashing sound. Eliana rolled off the bed in the side of the igloo she had made and crawled out through the small door. She stood up and looked around. One whole wall of the courtyard had been blasted to bits. And strangely enough, there were bits of fog surrounding it.

Eliana had noticed this, but she was still half asleep and didn't really care. Eliana was very thirsty, and since her power was water she sensed it was nearby. Eliana followed the tingling feeling in her chest out of the courtyard and into a small patch of trees. She walked through the trees gazing at all the different types of mushrooms, moss and plants that all grew around their trunks. Finally Eliana came upon a river. She kneeled down and drank the water greedily.

After Eliana had drank her fill she slipped into the cool water and felt it rush past her. Then she heard a splash. She looked up; a dark shape under the water was swimming towards her. Eliana was about to jump out of the river when a head popped out of the water. It was a mertoid man. He had light golden colored hair, blue green eyes, and a mischievous smile.

"Your Highness." He said.

"Umm, hi." Eliana said. "Who are you?"

"I am Warthon, a mertoid." Warthon answered. "I was just swimming out to the ocean."

"This river leads to the ocean?" Eliana said.

"Yes. There are many wonderful treasures buried there. I wanted to see what I could find. So what brings you to the river?"

"I was thirsty." Eliana replied. "And I wanted to cool off."

"Yes, you will need as much relaxing time as you can get before you save Etarfia."

"UGG! Don't remind me!" Eliana said. "I am so not looking forward to fighting an evil witch."

"Oh, many apologies." Warthon said.

Eliana stared at him. She smiled "Don't worry about it." She said.

Warthon looked around. "Are you here alone?"

"Yes." Eliana answered.

"You should not be here unprotected." Warthon held up the spear he had been carrying.

"I can take care of myself!" Eliana said. "I've even fought off a leopard seal! Well sort of fought off a leopard seal." she gave a meek smile.

Changing the subject Warthon said "You should turn yourself into a mertoid! Then we can go to the ocean and look for treasure together!"

"Can I do that?" Eliana asked with wide eyes.

"I believe so." Warthon answered.

"Umm, I don't know how." Eliana said.

Warthon thought "Concentrate really hard, and remember, you are the Queen of water."

"Alright, here goes." Eliana closed her eyes and cleared her mind, she only thought of having a tail. When she opened her eyes water was whirling around her waist and legs.

"You're doing it!" Warthon cried happily.

Eliana closed her eyes again. This time there was an explosion of blue light, when it dimmed in place of Eliana's legs there was a beautiful mertoid tail. It had nine flippers and had light blue, blue, dark blue, pink, and purple scales.

Eliana smiled. "Let's go!" she said.

But just as the two mertoid's were about to swim off, Latopa, Rostoa, Safferstar, and Katrina burst through the trees. They all had either a worried or angry look on their faces.

"What's wrong?" Eliana asked.

"What's wrong!?" Katrina shouted. "What's wrong!? Huliona and Hatara have not returned, Clerice and Cira have disappeared and you woke up first and didn't tell us!"

Eliana did not know what to say. Safferstar looked sick with worry and Rostoa, Latopa and Katrina looked fuming mad.

"Well, Hatara went to find Huliona so they are probably okay." Eliana said.

"What about Cira and Clerice?!" Rostoa roared.

"Why are you all made at me!?" Eliana said.

"Because!" Latopa cried. "You woke up first and didn't tell us they were gone!"

"I, I…" Eliana stuttered.

"Well," Katrina interrupted. "The important thing is that we find them, and fast!"

Chapter 23

NO HOPE

Huliona and Hatara peered over the side of the pool. They had walked over to the pool after the path leading to it had cleared. They wanted to see what it was going to do.

"Well nothing is happening." Hatara said.

"Just wait." Huliona answered.

"Guys come on; this is a really dangerous thing to do." Moyan said in a pleading tone.

"Look!" Hatara cried out. "It's misting over!"

Indeed the top of the pools glassy surface was misting over. The girls watched in excitement as the mist cleared and a picture started to form.

The picture was of Hatara and her brothers. They were running around in a field chasing her. Hatara laughing, fell in a heap onto the ground her smallest brother, Mathias landed on top of her then rolled into the grass laughing as hard as she was. A tear rolled down Hatara's cheek. It fell through the air and landed in the pool. Its surface rippled, changing the picture.

This time it was Huliona and her parents. Huliona gasped. In the picture Huliona was sitting with them down by the river she used to play at. Her mother was braiding her hair and her father looked to be telling a story. In the picture Huliona laughed. Then slowly the picture faded away. The only thing left in the pool was the girls' reflections.

"I think we should go." Moyan said.

"Okay." Both girls agreed, wiping tears from their eyes.

The three of them turned to leave, then suddenly without warning water shot from the pool and wrapped around Hatara's ankle. Hatara screamed.

"HATARA!" Huliona yelled.

The water yanked Hatara off her feet and with powerful strength dragged her towards the pool. Huliona lunged for Hatara; she grabbed her arm and started to pull. Hatara grabbed Huliona's arm with her other hand and started to flap her wings as hard as she could. But no matter how hard Huliona pulled or how hard Hatara flapped her wings the water would not let go.

The water pulled harder. This time it yanked Huliona off her feet. Then the water dragged Hatara into the pool. Huliona still hanging on was dragged into the water only half way, so she had enough time to grab a tree root that was sticking out of the ground.

"Moyan!" she screamed. "Go find the others!"

"What others!?" Moyan yelled franticly.

"The other Queens! Follow the path Hatara and I came out of until you find a courtyard! You will find them there! AHH!!" Huliona yelled as the water pulled harder

"I will not fail my Queen!" Moyan said as she raced into the forest.

The water lashed out again almost making Huliona loose her grip on the root. Recovering, Huliona knew Hatara would drown if she did not get her above the water. Huliona moved her hand down Hatara's arm. Then she wrapped her arm around Hatara right under her rib cage and with all her strength hoisted Hatara's head above the water.

Hatara's eyes were wide with fear. "Huliona!" she yelled. "What are we going to do!?"

"I sent Moyan to get the others! They will save us!" Huliona yelled over the roaring water.

Suddenly the girls heard a loud snapping sound. They looked up in horror as the tree root Huliona was hanging onto started to break.

"NO!!!" they shouted as the tree root snapped.

Huliona shot a vine out of her hand. It wrapped around a tree. The vine was now the only thing keeping both girls above the water.

Hatara!" Huliona shouted. "I'm sorry!"

"Sorry for what!?" Hatara yelled.

"If I had not run off none of this would have happened! We would be safe and maybe even home!" Huliona shouted.

"You must not blame yourself!"

"Hatara this is my fault and I'm sorry!"

Just as the girls noticed Huliona's vine was giving way Hatara said, "I forgive you."

Then the vine snapped, and both Queens were sucked under the pools dark water.

****

The girls were pulled far down into the pool. The current was fierce but the girls fought to reach the surface anyway, their lungs burning. At one point Huliona was almost sucked into another part of the pools deep chasm, but Hatara had grabbed her hand just in time. Eventually the girls stopped fighting, giving up hope. The current was much too strong. They were tossed like ragdolls all over the place.

Huliona's lungs were burning more than ever now, she thought she was going to pass out when someone put an air bubble on her head. Huliona could breathe! Hulona looked over at Hatara; she was pulling air from the water! Hatara made a second air bubble and put it on her own head.

"I don't know how long they will last!" Hatara yelled. Her voice sounded strange underwater.

The two girls decided that now that they could breathe they should try to get to the surface again. They started to fight the currant. But suddenly Huliona felt faint, Hatara's air bubble was going to pop. Huliona could tell Hatara knew too for she looked pale.

"The bubbles are going to pop!" Hatara yelled.

The two girls grabbed each others hands, waiting for the end. They had fought all they could. Then Huliona noticed something. There was a dark shape that almost looked like a person swimming towards her and Hatara. Huliona squinted, and just as her air bubble popped she made out who the person was.

Chapter 24

A CHOICE

Clerice, Cira and Moyan reached the wall of the courtyard.

"How are we going to get out?" Cira asked. "Safferstar and Katrina blocked off all the exits."

"We fly over of course!" Moyan said.

"Umm, there is only one small problem with that." Clerice said. "We can't fly!"

"Oh, yes." Moyan said. "I don't think I have enough magic to make it so you two can fly."

Cira sighed. "So what are we going to do!?"

"Keep it down!" Clerice said. "We don't want to wake up the others. Besides, I know how we can get out. I really hope this works."

Clerice took in a deep breath; she then thrust her hand towards the wall. A powerful fog shot out of Clerice's hands and hit the wall full force. Bits of rock and dust flew everywhere. Cira and Clerice ducked down and Moyan took cover behind a bush. After the rock shower ended the girls stood up and Moyan flew back over to them. As the dust settled the girls saw a huge gapping hole in the wall.

"So much for not waking everyone up!" Cira said.

Clerice looked around. "I don't think anyone did wake up. And that was the only thing I could think of."

"Okay, okay. Well at least it worked." Cira said. "Moyan, lead the way."

The fairy flew through the hole, the two young Queens following. They were in a sort of hallway. There were bugs and decaying rafters everywhere. Cira narrowly missed one as it fell from above.

"Uggg!" Cira said. "How did Huliona and Hatara even make it through here alive!?"

"No idea!" Clerice said, eyeing a particularly large spider.

Finally they came to the end of the hallway and stepped into the Gable Night Forest.

"This way!" Moyan said as she flew into the dark.

The girls ran after her. Once they caught up, they saw Moyan was hovering in front of a wall of roots and trees.

"This is the wall the forest made so we could not leave." Moyan said.

"Can trees really move here?" Clerice asked.

"Yes." Moyan said. "Especially the trees in this forest. The Gable Night Forest is very tricky. Now we must hurry!"

"Right!" Cira said. "I got this!"

Cira closed her eyes. When she opened them they were glowing a fierce gold. She thrust her hands forward. Fire shot from them and onto the roots and trees. The fire was on the roots and trees for less than a minute and it had already burned a hole in them. The three of them stepped through the hole and onto the path leading to the Misting Memory Pool.

"The path!" Moyan cried as she flew out of the hole.

The girls sped down the path, Moyan flying close behind. But when they reached the pool Clerice knew what she had been thinking was true, Huliona and Hatara had been sucked into the Misting Memory Pool. Clerice had a horrible sick feeling in her stomach. Just then the pool started to mist over. "I don't think so!" Cira screamed. She picked up a stone near by and chucked it into the pool, breaking the picture that had been forming. She turned to Clerice tears streaming down her face. "What are we going to do?"

Clerice was now crying as well. "I, I don't know."

****

Eliana stared back at her friends. "Um, I don't know how to change back."

"That won't be a problem." Latopa said. Suddenly Latopa started to glow the crimson color of her gem. Then her arms transformed into the arms of an ape. She then picked Eliana up out of the water and threw her over her shoulder.

"Now, let's go." Katrina said.

"Eliana waved to Warthon as she left. "I'm sorry!" she called. "But I must find my friends."

"I know Queen Eliana." Warthon said.

"Goodbye!" she called.

"Okay. We are going to start looking back at the courtyard." Katrina said. "We should be able to find some clues around the gaping hole in the wall."

"There's a hole in the…" Eliana started to say. "Oh, yeah."

"Yes you should know." Rostoa said.

"Hey!" Eliana snapped. "I'm sorry! I don't know why I didn't care there was a hole in the wall, but being mean to me and acting like I did this on purpose is not going to help!"

"Yes, Rostoa cut it out." Katrina said. "We know Eliana screwed up and we need to get over it."

Eliana was just about to shoot an insult back at Katrina when Latopa put an ape hand over her mouth. "Just let it go." She said. "We know you're sorry. Right everyone."

Rostoa mumbled a yes and Katrina agreed as well. At that moment they emerged from the small patch of trees they had been walking through and started along the side of the courtyard wall.

"Safferstar, you have not said a word, are you okay?" Rostoa asked.

"It was my job!" Safferstar wailed.

"What? What was your job?" Rostoa said.

"It was my job to protect all of you, and I did not!"

"Safferstar what nonsense!" Eliana said. "You have protected us! What happened was not your fault! It was ours. We will find the others and bring them back safely."

"Yes, everything will be fine." Latopa said.

They all stopped. They had reached the hole in the wall.

"Clerice did this." Rostoa said. "There is fog everywhere."

"Look," Katrina said. "The grass is trampled a lot over here. They must have gone this way."

"Come on, let's follow the path." Latopa said.

All of them followed the path of trampled grass. They followed the trampled grass into the hallway and into the Gable Night forest. They came to the spot where the roots and trees had blocked off the path so Huliona and Hatara could not leave.

"Cira must have done this." Latopa said, observing the singed edges of the roots and trees.

"What were they up too?" Katrina said as they all stepped through the hole.

Once they were through the hole everyone saw the path leading to the Misting Memory Pool. They looked to the end of the path and saw a large pool. In front of the pool Cira and Clerice stood talking in frantic voices. A fairy was hovering nearby. They all knew immediately something was wrong.

"Oh, you're safe!!" Safferstar cried as she ran towards Cira and Clerice.

The others followed. Once they had all reached the two girls at the pools edge they saw how pale they were, and their eyes were red from crying.

"What's wrong?" Katrina immediately asked.

"It, its Hatara and Huliona." Cira said.

"Where are they?" Rostoa asked in a worried tone.

Clerice pointed to the pool.

"NOOO!!!" Safferstar yelled. "No! Not a Misting Memory Pool!!"

This time the fairy spoke. "I am Moyan, a moonbeam fairy." She said in a sad tone. "I'm so sorry. I tried to reach you sooner."

"We are very grateful that you reached us at all." Katrina said with a nod.

"Oh what are we going to do!?" Latopa cried.

"I will go in after them." Eliana said.

"No," Safferstar said. "absolutely not."

"I'm the only one that can save them and we all know it. Besides, they are two of my very best friends and we can't save Etarfia without them." Eliana said.

There was a long pause. "Okay." Safferstar said. "But be carful. Go ahead Latopa."

All the girls gathered around the Misting Memory Pool. "We believe in you Eliana." Clerice said.

"Thanks." Eliana smiled. "Best friends forever."

"Best friends forever." The others said together.

"Now, Latopa throw me in."

"Good luck." Latopa said. And with one last look at her friend she threw Eliana into the pool.

****

Eliana immediately saw two black specks deep below her. She mustered up all her courage and started to swim. Eliana swam as fast as she could towards the specks. She knew she could never have done it without her tail. She thought of Warthon. She would have to thank him for telling her how to turn into a mertoid.

Eliana got closer and closer. Finally she could make the two specks out. The one on the left was Hatara and the one on the right was Huliona. They were still alive. But Hatara had passed out. She swam faster towards them. She saw Huliona had just seen her but then she passed out as well. Eliana finally reached them.

Eliana grabbed both girls around their waists. Then she mustered up all her power and…Eliana shot through the water. She was moving through the pool towards the surface and she wasn't even swimming! Only seconds later she broke the surface of the pool.

Everyone cried out in joy. Latopa lifted all three girls out of the pool with her ape arms. Katrina and Cira were going to give Huliona and Hatara CPR, but just before they could the two girls slowly opened their eyes.

Chapter 25

THE PALACE

The minute Hatara opened her eyes she started to throw up water. A couple of seconds later Huliona did the same.

"Oh, dear!" Safferstar cried. She snapped her fingers and two towels appeared. She gave one to Hatara and the other to Huliona.

"Are you two okay?" Latopa asked.

"Yeah, thanks to Eliana." The two girls smiled at Eliana gratefully.

Huliona looked over at Rostoa. Rostoa looked down. "I'm sorry Huliona." She said. "We should never have fought like that."

"I'm sorry too. It goes to show you, never leave someone angry, you never know if something bad may happen." Huliona said.

"I don't know what I would have done if, if…" Rostoa trailed off.

"I don't know what I would do without you either." Huliona said. The two cousins hugged.

"Okay, now that everyone has made up and been saved, we need to get back to the palace, Nathlene will be waiting." Katrina said.

"Who's Nathlene?" Hatara asked.

"She is the person currently in charge of Etarfia, or was in charge of Etarfia, now you girls are." Safferstar told them.

"Wow! I can't believe we are actually in charge of a whole magical land!" Rostoa said.

"Me either." The others agreed.

"Right, let's go. Latopa grab Eliana." Katrina said.

Latopa bent down and picked up Eliana once more. She put her over her shoulder.

"Are you sure you can't change back?" Latopa asked.

"No." Eliana said. "I tried while we were looking for the others but I couldn't."

"That's weird. I can change my arms back."

"Maybe our powers work differently."

"It is not a very long walk to the palace. Once we get there all of you can get a good meal and rest up. Then I will start to train you." Katrina told them.

"Train us?" Huliona questioned.

"Yes. I will teach you how to fight with a sword and how to use your powers properly." Katrina answered.

"Oh."

And with that said the party of nine walked back into the woods.

****

"Theses woods seem to go on forever!" Cira complained.

"Yeah." Clerice agreed. "My feet are killing me!"

"I thought you said it was not a long walk." Rostoa said.

"It's not." Katrina said. "The palace is right through those trees."

"Hey," Hatara said. "Where's Moyan?"

The others looked around. "I don't know." Latopa said. "I didn't see her leave with us."

"She probably went home." Safferstar said. "Fairies consider themselves very busy creatures. They don't like to dottle."

Just then Katrina disappeared behind a big clump of trees.

"Hey, wait up!" Eliana yelled as the others ran to follow.

When the girls emerged from the clump of trees next to Katrina the sight they saw took their breath away. What the girls saw was a large sparkling lake. On the far bank of the lake sat a huge palace shining in the early moonlight. And behind that were forests and mountains as far as the eye could see.

Chapter 26

NATHLENE

The girls walked along the edge of the lake towards a barge floating about ten feet into the water.

"Guys! Look!" Huliona said pointing across the water.

All the girls looked to where Huliona was pointing and gasped. There were big and small lily pads floating on the water and on them sat all types of creatures. Frogs with wings, regular frogs, tiny mermaids with long scaly tails, water pixies up to their own tricks. The girls couldn't believe their eyes.

"A lot of different creatures live in this lake." Safferstar said quietly. "But be quiet. They don't take kindly to noise."

The girls nodded eyes wide. "Did these creatures used to be humans too?" Cira asked.

"Some, but not all. Most are the people who turned into theses beings' children." Safferstar answered.

"They're lovely." Latopa said gazing at one of the water pixies.

"Come!" Katrina said to them. "You can look at the water folk later, we have to get moving."

"We're coming we're coming." Eliana said as they headed over to the barge."

As they neared the barge they saw a light person was waiting for them fluffing the cushions on the barge seats. When she saw the group approaching her she quickly stopped what she was doing and stood up strait.

"Your highnesses." She said bowing deeply. "I am Clover, a light person. I work on this barge."

"Hi Clover." The others said.

"Ah, Queen Latopa, I am glad to see the sabberon did not harm you." Clover said.

"Thank you. So am I." Latopa said.

Clover smiled, but when she noticed Eliana she giggled a little. "Queen Eliana I see you have started to experiment with your powers." Clover pointed to Eliana's tail.

Eliana smiled. "It's a long story." She said.

"Oh!" Clover suddenly cried out. "Queen Cira! Is it really you?"

Cira smiled. "The one and only." She said.

"Oh, gracious Queen Cira I would be honored to fight beside you in battle."

"Oh, um, uhhh…" not really knowing what to say Cira looked over at Safferstar.

"Umm Clover the girls are not really ready for battle yet." Safferstar said.

"Oh yes. How foolish of me." Clover said. "My apologies."

"Oh it's no big deal." Cira said.

After Katrina and Safferstar talked to Clover a little longer about how late the barge would be operating they all boarded the barge. Once everyone was seated Clover closed the barge gate.

"Is everyone comfortable?" she asked.

"Yes." All of them chorused.

"Okay then, let's go!" Clover then started the barge and headed out onto the lake.

All the girls looked over the side of the barge and watched the water. It twinkled and sparkled in the moonlight. They even saw fairy dust floating above the water.

"It's so beautiful!" Latopa whispered.

"Isn't it." Rostoa agreed.

"Hey!" Hatara exclaimed. "Look!" Hatara pointed across the water. All the girls looked in the direction Hatara was pointing.

There was a large rock sticking out of the water, and on the rock a mertoid sat singing.

"She's so glamorous!" Clerice exclaimed.

"A lot of mertoids live in this lake." Katrina told her.

"What's the lake called?" Cira asked.

"The lake of Dreams and Sorrow."

"Well that's a dumb name!" Cira said. "That's sad, why would someone name the lake that?"

"Well, a lot of dreams have come true at this lake and a lot of dreams are destroyed here." Katrina answered.

"Well that only emphasizes my point." Cira said.

"I'm with you on that one." Huliona agreed.

"I wonder if we can change the name." Hatara wondered aloud.

"Oh, well I don't like the name either," Rostoa said. "But I don't think it would be right to change it."

"Me either." Latopa said. "It was part of Etarfia long before we got here."

"I suppose your right." Hatara said.

Talk then carried on to other things and finally after about ten more minutes the barge reached the other side of the lake. Clover opened the barge door, a golden platform extended over the water that was too shallow for the barge and ended right where the water met land. Everyone walked across the platform and onto land.

"Thank you clover."Clerice said.

"Yes thank you very much Clover." Safferstar said.

Clover nodded and smiled. She walked back onto her barge while the others headed into the palace. Well almost everyone. Huliona had hung back, she had just seen part of what looked to be a large garden and wanted to check it out. So Huliona slipped away from the others and trotted along the castle wall until she came to a corner.

Huliona stopped short, around the corner was the most beautiful array of gardens she had ever seen! It had flowers all colors of the rainbow; some even glowed in the dark! There were rose's, pansies, daisies, carnations, endless types of flowers. And almost everywhere fountains with big coy-fish swimming in them sprayed up around the flowers. And on the fountains and in flower beds were beautiful statues.

Huliona was twirling in circles trying to take in all the beauty at once. She noticed a rose bush with the biggest roses she had ever seen. She walked over to it and stuck her nose into one of the yellow roses, breathing in deeply.

"Enjoying the garden?" a voice said.

Huliona whirled around. A mushroom person was standing not far off, leaning against a tree. He looked young thirteen or so. He had deep brown eyes and he had a friendly smile.

"Oh, um yes." Huliona sputtered, blushing.

"Did I startle you?" He asked, looking concerned.

"Oh, a little. But I'm fine." Huliona quickly said.

"Many apologies." He said. "I am Catton, a mushroom person."

"Hi. I'm, well," Huliona wasn't sure if she should address herself as a Queen. "I am Queen Huliona." She finally said.

Catton smiled. "Yes, everyone is talking about how the seven Queens have come."

****

"The palace is so beautiful!" Latopa exclaimed.

The girls had just walked into the huge palace and were now marveling at its beauty. The room the girls were in now had a floor made of a sandy colored marble. Then to the back of the room was a large white marble staircase. In all four corners of the room stood large pillars. In front of each pillar was a crystal table. Sitting on each table were tall lupines in diamond vases. And the whole room had real flower garlands hanging from the walls which were an off white color. They reached all the way to the top of the very high ceiling.

"This is the grand foyer." Safferstar told them.

"Hey, where's Huliona?" Clerice asked.

"Not again!" Rostoa moaned.

"I'll find her." Latopa said.

"I'm coming with you." Katrina said. "We can't risk any more accidents."

"Oh! I want to come too!" Eliana said.

"No," Katrina said. "You're still turning back to normal."

Latopa put Eliana down on the marble floor then turned her arms back to normal. Then she and Katrina strode out of the palace doors.

"I think I hear her talking." Latopa said, running along the palace wall.

"So do I." Katrina said following close behind.

They followed the voice along the castle wall all the way to the corner. The two found her in a huge garden talking to a mushroom person. Huliona looked up.

"What for Etarfia's sake are you doing now!?" Katrina asked in a tired and annoyed tone.

"I was," Huliona started to say.

"You should not have wandered off!" Katrina interrupted.

"I'm sorry!!" Huliona said loudly, now she was annoyed. "I saw part of the garden and I wanted to look at it."

"Well let me know first!" Katrina said throwing up her hands. "We have had too many accidents." Katrina then turned to Catton. "Catton, you should be with Nathlene." She said. "I don't know why you're out here."

"Yes Captain Katrina." Catton said. "Many apologies I will go now." Catton then turned to Huliona and Latopa; he bowed then ran back towards the palace.

"Why would Nathlene need him?" Huliona asked.

"He is a servant." Katrina said plainly.

"What, a servant?" Huliona said.

"Yes, a servant, they are expected to do their duties." Katrina said.

"Oh." Huliona said.

"Come on lets go in." Latopa said. "I'm getting cold."

"Yes come. The others will be worried." Katrina said.

So they all left the garden and headed back into the palace.

****

Once they reached the palace the three girls found a woman talking to the others, and Catton was with her. She was not very tall but she was petite with a light tan skin color and soft brown curls. When the woman saw the girls coming she smiled warmly.

"Greeting's my Queen's!" She said. "What an honor to finally meet you! I am Nathlene." Nathlene bowed.

"You too." Huliona said.

"I am so glad you have come! You must be tired from your journey." Nathlene said. "In fact I was just telling the other Queen's were your sleeping quarters are."

"Oh," Latopa said. "Thank you, we are very tired."

"Come, I will show you all to your rooms." Nathlene said as she headed towards the marble staircase. The others followed close behind.

When Nathlene was far enough up the stairs and talking to Eliana who had legs again Latopa, knowing Nathlene could not here her leaned over to Huliona and whispered "There is something fishy about her."

"I know." Huliona answered. "I sensed it when I walked in."

Chapter 27

TRAINING

Huliona opened her eyes. Light streamed in from the open window. The night before Nathlene had shown the girls their rooms. They had all fallen into bed, exhausted from all the events that had occurred. Huliona had barely gotten a good look at her room. But now she saw it clearly and she loved it.

Huliona's bed was a hammock made out of a giant soft leave. Soft pillows and blankets made of silk and dandelion fluff littered the bed. Next to her bed was a mushroom side table with a comb made of sticks along with other oddball items. Across the room was a mahogany desk with a mushroom stool. But what was in the middle of the room was the best of all. In the center of Huliona's room sat a giant tree. Its branches covered in rich green leaves sprayed across the ceiling making the room look like a forest. In the trees trunk were drawers to put clothes. And in the middle of the tree, at the very top, was a flat surface where two chairs and a table sat with a vase of flowers on it.

Huliona looked around her room in wonder once more taking it all in. This was one of the most amazing things she had ever seen!

Huliona then glanced at the clock, "Nine o'clock!" she exclaimed. "I slept late!" she jumped out of bed and walked across the moss covered floor over to the tree. She riffled through the fully stocked drawers looking for something to wear. She finally decided on cotton pants and a long sleeved sage green top with flower embroidery on the front.

Huliona was about to pick up the brush to brush her hair when Hatara burst into her room, tears streaming down her face.

Huliona's stomach instantly twisted. "What is it?" she cried.

"Its Moyan," Hatara sobbed. "She's been attacked."

Huliona raced out of her room after Hatara. The two flew down the hallway towards the stairs. They bumped into the others on the way down.

"What happened!?" Latopa cried. She had just woken up herself and her hair was everywhere.

"Moyan has been attacked." Huliona answered.

"Oh no!" Latopa said, increasing her speed.

The seven girls ran outside and down the stone path in the front of the palace. The small fairy was lying on her stomach on the cold stone. Safferstar, Katrina, Catton, Nathlene, Clover and some other cloud people the girls didn't know, were all gathered around her. All of them looked very worried.

"Oh dear!" Clerice exclaimed.

"Oh!" Cira gasped next.

Moyan was a horrid sight. Her wings were shredded and her hair was out of its neat curly bun. Her shoes were gone, her skin had dirt smudges everywhere, and her dress was so badly torn it was almost falling off.

"Who did this!!!" Eliana raged.

Moyan lifted her head, "The Pixsries."

"What are Pixsries?" Rostoa asked.

"Evil pixies." Clover told her.

Hatara reached down and carefully picked Moyan up. She placed her in her hand. "Tell us what happened." She said wiping tears from her eyes.

"Well," Moyan sputtered. "back at the misting memory pool when you all were talking I saw some bushes rustle behind you. Then something flew out of them and into the wood, so I followed it. I had been following it for a good twenty minutes when I knew it had sensed me. I ducked behind a tree just as it turned around. I then saw it was a pixrie, and it had seen me. It gave a high pitched scream. Then in minutes other pixries flew out of the shadows from every direction." Moyan shuddered, and then continued. "The pixries surrounded me. But when I tried to escape they attacked me. They tore my dress and wings, hit me. Then just when I thought all hope was lost I saw pink lights starting to appear in the distance. When the pink lights got closer they seemed to have noticed me, because they started speeding towards me and the pixries. As the pink lights dimmed I saw they were petal pixies. Good pixies. They attacked the pixries and started to pull them off me. Then as you may guess the pixries forgot all about me and started to fight the petal pixies. But once the pixries let go of me I started to fall. I couldn't fly because my wings were too badly shredded. I believe it was the lead scout of the petal pixies who caught me. He sprinkled me with pixie dust and told me to get away wile I could. I thanked him, and then I ran. And the last thing I saw was the petal pixies chasing after the pixries who were retreating." Moyan finished.

"Horrah for petal pixies!" Clerice cheered.

Everyone cheered in agreement. Everyone that is, except for Nathlene, she looked mad. "Safferstar!" Nathlene snapped.

"Take Rate and Throrta. Go search for any wounded pixries or petal pixies. Bring them back."

Safferstar looked taken aback by Nathlene's sharp tone, but nodded and motioned for the two cloud people to follow her. They started to walk away.

"Wait!" Huliona said. "We will come with you." She started to follow Safferstar, the others close behind.

"No!" Nathlene said.

Huliona turned surprised. "And just why not?" Eliana said.

"You are needed here." Nathlene said, trying to backpetal. She did not like the look Eliana was giving her.

"Nathlene," Hatara said. "This was an attack, without warning on an unarmed fairy, we cannot let this go!"

"Yes," said Cira. "We are not going to stay here while we send others out into danger. There could be more pixries."

"No girls really, its fine." Safferstar said gently. "I have magic too don't forget. And Rate and Throrta are trained fighters." Safferstar gave the girls a pleading look.

Latopa narrowed her eyes to slits. She looked over at Nathlene, she hated her already. "Okay," she said. "Just be careful." She turned to Safferstar.

"Yes, let us know if you need help or if you find anything." Rostoa said, grabbing Eliana's arm and pulling her towards the palace, she looked as if she was going to throttle someone.

Katrina, looking nervous walked over to Hatara. "I am going to take her to the doctor." She said, picking up Moyan. "I will call for you in an hour to start your training." With that Katrina strode off in the direction of the barge with Clover at her side.

"What should we do now?" Cira asked. They were all inside the palace once more, standing in the entrance hall.

"Hmmmm," Huliona said. "We are the Queens of a magical land and we have a palace all to ourselves, and strangely I can't think of anything!"

Everyone laughed. "Hey," Latopa said. "I have an idea; we can show each other our rooms!"

"Oh that's a great idea!" Rostoa said. "I can't wait for you to see mine."

The girls all agreed, and then set off up the long marble stair case. "Uggg!" Clerice groaned once she reached the top. "My thighs are burning!"

"Mine too!" Huiona said. "You would think they would have a magic carpet or something!"

"Right you are!" Rostoa said as she crawled the rest of the way up.

"Oh come on girls!" Eliana said. "It wasn't that bad! Stay in good spirits. Hey we can even see my room first."

"Easy for you to say!" Latopa said. "You reached the top first."

"Come on guys, let's go." Clerice said. "We don't want to waste all our time here."

The girls headed down the hall to Eliana's room. Eliana opened her door. "Oh!" Cira exclaimed. "It's beautiful!"

"Thanks!" Eliana said.

Eliana's bed was made out of a giant clam shell that opened and closed. It had fine blankets and pillows made of driftwood and sea grass fibers resting on the soft mattress. Next to the bed was a driftwood bed table. Across the room was a wardrobe made out of giant muscle shells. Next to that was a vanity with a clam shell mirror and a sea glass top, it also had a chair made out of a wrecked ships bow. But the best thing was the water room. Up near the ceiling there was a loft like area, but it was all water! So Eliana was able to go in that small room and swim!

The girls marveled at Eliana's room for a while. "Let's go to my room!" Hatara said.

"Okay." The others agreed. So everyone left Eliana's room and headed over to Hatara's.

Once the girls entered Hatara's room they all gasped. Her whole room was a giant clear windmill! They could see right outside.

"Where's your furniture?" Cira asked looking around.

Hatara pointed to the ceiling. The girls looked up. All Hatara's furniture was floating in the air on small white clouds. Her bed was king size and had white and light blue bedding made of gypsy moth webs woven together. She also had many different wind chimes hanging over it. Her bed table and bureau and vanity were white. And her vanity had a big wind vane next to it that changed color.

The girls were just as impressed by Hatara's room as they were with Eliana's. And just as the girls left Hatara's room they heard Katrina calling them from downstairs. They ran down the marble staircase and out into the castle yard where Katrina was waiting for them.

"Ready for training?" She asked. Without waiting for a reply she said, "Good. Okay let's go." Katrina started towards the woods.

****

The girls followed Katrina along the castle wall towards the woods. They traveled through a small garden, in which a group of gnomes were conversing on how they should cook their rhubarb pie. They bowed as the girls passed. The girls smiled with delight and waved back. Next they walked through a hall in the woods with statues all along both sides. The girls gazed at the statues, wide eyed.

"Those are other heroes of Etarfia." Katrina told them.

"Wow." Huliona said gazing at a statue of a woman with flowing golden hair. She was about to ask Katrina who she was but she was too far ahead, she ran after the others.

Finally the girls reached a courtyard. In the courtyard sat seven things. A pile of rock, a pile of roots and grass, a mass of grey clouds, a large deer, a huge eagle, a pool of water and a ball of light.

"Let me introduce you to you're magic soul mates." Katrina said.

"What are magic soul mates?" Latopa asked, inspecting each of the seven things with interest.

"They are beings that are connected to your power almost as much as you. And they can help you understand it better." Katrina answered.

"Oh." The girls all said together, they were curious already.

"Now, Rostoa, this is Shantoro." The huge pile of rock suddenly turned into a rough looking rock bear. "Huliona this is Alrie." The pile of roots and grass turned into a horse with a flowing grass mane. "Clerice this is Mrenshoon." The mass of grey clouds suddenly turned into a huge cloud griffin with long curved talons. "Latopa this is Nightin." Katrina motioned to the deer.

"Hey!" Latopa exclaimed. "Are you the deer that saved me from the Sabberon?"

"I am." Nightin said proudly.

"Hatara, this is Frina." Katrina said as she motioned toward the giant eagle. "Eliana, this is Melark." The pool of water rose up into the form of a she wolf, her hair made of sparkling ice.

"And last but not least Cira, this is Yotru." The ball of light turned into a phoenix.

"Were they here even before we arrived?" Huliona asked.

"We have been here since the beginning of Etarfia Queen Huliona." Alrie said.

"It was always our destiny to be connected with the future Queens of Etarfia." Mrenshoon said. "So we were created along with when the magic took over the island, to wait for your arrival."

The girls were in awe they greeted all of the magic soul mates, getting to know them better.

"Okay, now that we are all acquainted, lets start training." Katrina said.

****

"Let's start with you Rostoa." Katrina said.

Rostoa, looking nervous stepped forward and tentatively made her way over to Katrina.

"Try and move that rock." Katrina said, pointing to a medium sized boulder.

Rostoa, seeing the size of the rock, smiled. "This'll be a cinch." She said to the others. Rostoa headed over to the boulder and stood about ten feet away from it. She then started to pull her hands toward her, nothing happened for a second, but then without warning the rock blew up.

The girls, with screams of surprise, ducked as Shantoro ran forward. He turned into a huge rock wall that blocked the chunks of rock from hitting everyone.

"Oh!" Rostoa groaned red in the face.

"No, no, it's okay!" Katrina said. "Great first try."

Everyone including Rostoa looked at Katrina as if she were crazy.

"You have got to be kidding me!" Rostoa said. "I almost killed everyone!"

"Yes, but at least the rock did something." Katrina answered.

"But I was able to move those rocks at the other courtyard. Why can't I move that rock?" Rostoa asked.

"I think you were more determined then that you are now." Shantoro growled.

"Shantoro is right, you need to really be determined to do something when you are first trying out. It helps focus your magic and power." Katrina said. "Okay, Shantoro, go help Rostoa practice over there. I want to see what Cira can do."

Cira approached Katrina. "I want you to make a ball of light. And remember, concentrate." Cira nodded.

Cira closed her eyes and cleared her mind. She then cupped her hands together. After a few moments Cira opened her eyes and uncupped her hands. A ball of light was floating there, a perfect sphere.

"Excellent!" Katrina cried. Everyone clapped and cried out congratulations. Cira blushed.

"Huliona, your next."

Huliona approached Katrina, feeling confident.

"Huliona, make a cherry tree grow out of the ground. Now this will take real concentration, so do not get distracted." Katrina said.

"Okay." Huliona said. She knelt down and put her hands on the ground and closed her eyes. Everyone felt the ground shake; suddenly a huge apple tree grew out of the ground.

"Katrina laughed. "A cherry tree Huliona, a cherry tree."

"Oh." Huliona said laughing. The others laughed too and clapped. She then reached up and plucked an apple off one of the low branches. She bit into it, juice dribbled down her chin. "Itsss sweettt." She said here mouth full.

Katrina laughed. Great job!" she said. "Okay, Clerice you're up!"

Chapter 28

WHO THEY ARE

A lone sabberon stood in the middle of a large field. The sun was beating down heavily and he was frustrated. He sniffed the air then cursed quietly to himself. Just the day before he had had the scent of those blasted queens, now it had left him. He snarled, if he had only gotten to kill that one queen he would have enough of her sent to last for days. Then he could find the others.

He looked up; something had just glinted in the sun. He squinted his eyes, and then smiled displaying his sharp teeth. It was a phoenix, soaring through the air. And he knew exactly where it was going.

****

Hatara grabbed a brownie from the crystal platter sitting on the dinning room table. She stuffed it into her mouth and chewed with content. The girls had been in Etarfia for about a week now and had been perfecting their powers. They could now do things they had never dreamed of. But they were tired, and a little anxious, for the battle was getting closer every day.

Now they sat at the dinning room table, eating a snack before one of their particularly long days.

"Man am I tired!" Eliana announced as she entered the room.

"So am I." Latopa agreed.

"I'm not too tired." Hatara said as she yawned.

"But you just yawned." Huliona pointed out.

"Well I said I wasn't too tired, and besides that was a fake yawn." Hatara said.

"That was so not a fake yawn!" Huliona retorted.

"It was!"

"Oh, no it wasn't."

"Yes it…"

"Girls!" Nathlene screeched. Everyone jumped. Cira dropped her chocolate cake on the floor. "I am getting sick and tired of you arguing about the stupidest things! All the time!"

The girls did not like Nathlene. They liked the fact that they did not see her that much, but when they did she was always a bit nasty, and no one knew why.

"We are teenagers," Cira said trying to balance the fallen cake on her fork. "That's what we do. Besides we are the Queens, we can do whatever we like."

Nathlene's face turned a bright shade of red and she sucked in a deep breath.

"Cira!" Katrina said. "Do not talk to Nathlene that way!"

"Hey, she,"

"No!"

Cira scowled as she managed to get the cake back onto her plate. She then muttered something no one else could hear and jabbed at her bowl of tapioca pudding.

It was silent until Huliona asked, "Who are the evil witches?"

"I beg your pardon?" Safferstar asked.

"Like, what are their names, and personalities." Huliona answered.

"Oh." Safferstar said. "Well the first is Joycore. She is their leader, and the worst of them all."

Suddenly before Safferstar could get another word in Moyan flew through the door and into the dinning room. She flashed a brilliant smile.

"Moyan!" the girls cried. All of them jumped up from their seats and ran over to the small fairy.

"I'm so glad to see you!" Moyan cried.

"Dito!" Huliona said.

"Are you feeling better?" Latopa asked.

"Much better thank you." Moyan said. "I was taken to Belrane."

"What's Belrane?" Clerice asked.

"It is a small town near the middle of Etarfia. They have the best doctors there. They fixed me up in a jiffy!" Moyan smiled.

"Come sit down." Rostoa said. "We have Rhubarb pie. The gnomes make us some every morning."

"Yes." said Eliana. "And Safferstar was just telling us about the evil witches!"

"Id love to, but I'm afraid I can't stay. I have some important business to attend to." Moyan said, she put her hand next to her mouth and whispered, "Army business."

The girls laughed. "Oh, okay. Well see you later!"

Moyan waved to everyone then left the room. The girls returned to their seats.

"Alright." Safferstar said. "Now I didn't tell you girls this yet. But all the witches have the same powers you girls have."

"They have our powers!" Hatara cried.

"Well in a sense." Safferstar said. "They all have your powers, but they are opposites. Take Cira for example. Her fire and light is yellow and orange. Braysip, her Opposite has red fire."

"Oh I get it." Hatara said. "Their powers, are our powers, only they are evil. Our powers are good, but theirs are bad."

"Exactly. Joycore's power is animals. Then there is Moshtic. Her power is plants and fungus, evil of course. Capsa is weather. Acrim, evil rock and soil. Dase air and wind. And Krees water and ice."

"Yes," Katrina said, she seemed to be staring into space. "one for each of you."

The girls were silent. A shiver went down all their spines. Suddenly they heard crashes and screams from outside. The silent spell was broken; they all jumped up in alarm.

Suddenly Catton burst into the room; there was a large gash in his arm. "It's the sabberon," he gasped. "He has found you."

Chapter 29

TRUTH

The seven Queens ran from the dinning room. They sped through the entrance hall and outside. Yes, the sabberon was there. He had caused more damage than anyone could have imagined too. He had torn down many trees, smashed a fountain. Now he was pinning a unicorn named Esha to the ground. She bucked and neighed helplessly.

"Okay," Katrina said. "Let's see what your training has taught you." She looked at the girls. "You can do this."

Latopa turned into a huge tiger. She then ran forward and jumped into the air. She landed on the sabberon's back; she dug her six inch long claws into its sides. She then sprouted huge eagle wings; she lifted the sabberon into the air.

"That a girl Latopa!" Katrina shouted.

The sabberon yelped in pain as he was lifted off the unicorn and thrown. He hit the ground hard. He lay unconscious. Everyone cheered as Latopa turned back to normal beaming. But in all the commotion no one except Huliona noticed the sabberon get to his feet, shake himself and start running towards Latopa.

"Get out of the way!!" Huliona yelled. She ran forward.

Huliona pushed Latopa out of the way of the sabberon, and just in time. She quickly shot two thick vines out of her hands. They wrapped around each other for extra strength then wrapped around the sabberon's neck. The sabberon stopped, bewildered. As he struggled Huliona made her hands into a fists, which made the vines around the sabberons neck tighten.

"Help!" Huliona shouted. But Rostoa was already on her way.

Rostoa grabbed a huge boulder and lifted it over her shoulders. She whispered something to it then threw it into the air towards the sabberon. The boulder turned into a cage with bars of rough stone and no bottom. The cage landed on the sabberon, imprisoning him.

Everyone cheered. They jumped up and down hugging each other.

The sabberon laughed a horse dry laugh. "Celebrate while you can." He said. "The witches will finish you off soon enough."

Katrina rounded on him. "Silence." She hissed. Katrina walked right up to the bars of the cage and stuck her face in front of the sabberons. "How dare you come here and cause all this destruction." She said. "Your mistresses agreed to not send private attacks."

The sabberon smiled. "Well, I guess they didn't like that idea." He whispered.

Suddenly the ground started shaking. Nathlene had entered the yard, a rock giant following. The girl's jaws dropped. They looked up at the rock giant with wonder.

The rock giant looked down at them and smiled, but the moment he saw Rostoa he dropped to one knee and bowed. The girls tried to keep their balance for the ground had shaken even more that time. "My Queen Rostoa!" he bellowed. "And the other Queens of Etarfia as well, I am Nison, a rock giant."

"I can see that!" Rostoa giggled, still awestruck.

Nison laughed a loud joyful laugh. He had a friendly look to his face that all the girls immediately liked.

"Nison! Take the sabberon to the dungeon!" Nathlene said in a shrill voice.

"Geese." Clerice whispered in Huliona's ear. Huliona laughed.

Nison walked over to the sabberons cage. He picked it up and then started to carry it away. The girls could still hear the sabberons shouts and threats long after he was out of sight.

The unicorn that had been pinned to the ground then came into view; she had taken shelter behind a bush. She approached the girls. "Thank you so much my gracious Queens!" She said. "I am humble to be in your presence."

Huliona, Latopa, and Rostoa blushed.

"I am Esha, a unicorn." she said.

"What a lovely name!" Cira said.

"Why thank you Queen Cira!" Esha neighed.

"Yes and whenever you need us just call." Huliona said.

Esha smiled.

"Oh my! Look at the time!" Safferstar said glancing up at the sun. Etarfian's could tell the time of day by where the sun was. "Girls we must get going. I almost forgot about your battle armor fitting." Safferstar said.

"Okay." They said.

"Bye Esha!"

"See ya!"

"Talk to you soon!"

"Chao!"

All the girls shouted their goodbyes as they were hustled off towards the palace. Esha said goodbye as well then hurried off down the lane in the wood, on her own business. Soon Nathlene was the only one left in the yard.

Nathlene looked around; making sure no one was looking, and then slipped into the wood.

****

An evil witch sat on her thrown. She banged her fist down on the huge chair.

"Relax, Joycore." Acrim said.

"I cannot!" Joycore yelled, she was fuming mad. "How could those, those children get into Etarfia!? We blocked all the entryways and exits!"

"Why?" Acrim said. "Are you afraid of them? They are children as you said."

"No." Joycore hissed. "In fact I can't wait to crush them, and their hopes of ever seeing Etarfia free again."

"That's the spirit." Acrim said. "As for them getting into Etarfia, that sprite kin Safferstar went and got them. She has always bee troublesome, always rebelling."

"Not for long." Capsa said as she entered the room. "She will break. Especially if we keep sending attacks."

Suddenly Moshtic burst into the room, followed by Braysip and Krees.

"Those wretched Queens have captured our sabberon! Our sabberon!" Moshtic raged.

"What!?" Capsa cried. "This cannot be."

"But it is." Krees said. "It was only but twenty minutes ago."

"This is an outrage!" Acrim bellowed. "What a stupid sabberon."

"One of them put deep gashes in his sides, another almost strangled him, and the last nearly crushed the brut with a rock." Braysip said.

"Oh!" Acrim screamed "What are we going to do! He was our best fighter, and most loyal."

"Quiet!" Joycore shouted. "I have a plan. But I will tell you when Dase arrives. Where the devil is Dase anyway?"

"She is out going to fetch that Natin or whatever her name is." Krees said. "Apparently she has more news for us."

"She better." Moshtic sneered.

Just a few moments later Dase entered the room, followed by a frightened looking Nathlene.

****

"So, the traitor has arrived!" Acrim laughed wickedly. The others laughed as well.

"I heard you have brought us news." Joycore said, staring down at Nathlene with cold blue eyes.

"I have your darkness." Nathlene said looking at the floor.

Dase looked to be getting impatient. "Well pick your head up and tell us the news! We have been waiting all day!" She said.

"Oh, um, yes, well as your majesties know the sabberon has been captured." Nathlene said.

"Yes, we know." Braysip laughed wickedly.

"Well I think I know a way to free him." Nathlene said. "You see," she said, then looked around and took a deep breath. "The Queens are getting fitted for their battle armor right now, so they won't be around, as will Safferstar. Katrina will be cleaning up the mess the sabberon made. The guards will also do whatever I say. So it will be easy to free him." Nathlene finished quickly.

"Hmm..." Acrim said. "Very well. But bring him too us at sunset."

Nathlene turned to leave. "Wait!" Joycore said. "Just in case you fail, or even if you get the sabberon out of the dungeons," She paused. "Bring us a captive as well."

Nathlene gulped. "A, a captive your majesty?" She whispered.

"You know someone the girls or at least, one of the girls has grown to like. Now we will be equal, a captive for a captive. Or just a captive!" Joycore laughed.

"But..."

"You heard me, now go!"

Dase grabbed Nathlene's arm. She dragged her to the small castles door and shoved her out. "You know Nathlene," she said before she shut the door. "some people would think you are afraid of us." Then Dase smiled and the big redwood door was shut in Nathlene's face.

Nathlene mounted her horse and started the journey back to the palace. The entire way, she could not think of anyone except for Safferstar and Katrina, that the girls really liked. And she knew she could not take them. Then, she remembered Catton.

Chapter 30

GONE

The girls followed Safferstar into the palace and down a long hallway with a lot of doors on either side. Safferstar stopped at the very last door before the hallway branched off in two different directions. The door was huge, made of rich pine, and had a lot of fancy pictures carved into it by and unknown artist.

"This is where I leave you." Katrina said. "I need to start cleaning up that mess the sabberon made."

"Oh ya," Huliona said. "He really caused some damage."

"Also trying outfits on isn't really my thing." Katrina said. Everyone laughed. "Okay, bye everybody!"

"Bye Katrina!" the girls shouted after her.

"Alright girls, are you ready?" Safferstar said.

"Yes." Eliana said.

"Okay let's go." Safferstar then opened the huge pine door. The girls walked into a cylinder shaped room with a high ceiling. To the right and in the back of the room sat a circular platform with a mirror behind it. In the front of the room were two elegant red velvet chairs. In the middle of the chairs sat a small round coffee table with a vase of lupines on it. And beautiful tapestries hung on the walls.

The girls looked to the back of the room at another pine door. It had opened and a beautiful woman had stepped out. She had long dark red wavy hair, bright red lipstick and a dress on that was made out of long wide pieces of sea weed, and her sandals were made out of sand dollars.

She smiled and bowed. "Hi, I'm Colly." She said.

"What kind of magical being are you?" Eliana asked.

Colly laughed. "What magical being am I? I am a Water Sharillon."

"What's a Water Sharillon?" Huliona asked.

"A Water Sharillon is a being made completely out of water, but we can hold our shape. We can also control what water does." Colly told her.

"That's really cool!" Cira said.

"Okay," Colly said. "I hear you have come to get fitted for your battle armor."

"Yes they are." Safferstar said.

"Oh good! I just finished Huliona's this morning." Colly then ran into the back room. The girls heard some shuffling and something fall. Then Colly came out bearing seven huge velvet bags. She blew a piece of hair out of her face. "Whooo" she said. "I really have to clean up in there." She set the bags down. "Alright Eliana you're up!"

Eliana stepped onto the circular platform. Colly went to the second bag, the blue one and pulled out Eliana's battle armor. It was a light blue wrap dress. It ended at her knees and had a one shoulder strap with a small train in the back. Next she took out dark blue boots made of fish scales and a blue and white sea shell comb.

Eliana then took of the dress she had on so that she was only wearing her slip. Colly handed her the dress and Eliana slipped it on. She then pulled the boots on which were surprisingly comfortable.

"How does it fit?" Colly asked.

"Good, but my hair is in the way." Eliana said, she tried to push it out of the way, slightly frustraited.

"Oh, right!" Colly said as she grabbed the seashell comb. She took Eliana's hair and rolled it into the comb. "Better?"

"Much thanks." Eliana said. Eliana looked into the mirror. "It fits good and everything, but how is this dress going to protect me? No offense."

Colly ran from the room.

"Did I upset her?" Eliana asked looking worried.

"Not in the least!" Colly said returning. She had a bow and arrow with her. "I'll show you." Colly strung the arrow and let it fly. Thud, it hit Eliana but bounced right off. "It is material that resists any kind of metal."

Eliana looked terrified. "Oh," she said.

"Are you alright?" Colly asked.

"Yes, that was just scary." Eliana said recovering.

"Oh, you thought," Colly laughed. "No no Queen Eliana! I was only going to demonstrate the clothes strength. I was not mad!" Colly kept laughing. Then the girls started to laugh as well.

"Eliana," Rostoa said, you thought Colly was going to hurt you?"

"Well she ran from the room and came back with a bow and arrow!" Eliana cried in defense. But a smile was creeping across her face.

"Okay. Okay, we know what you mean." Safferstar said, still stifling giggles.

"Huliona your next!" Colly said.

Huliona then stepped onto the platform as Eliana changed back into her other dress. Colly then went to the green bag and took out a dress and sandals. The dress was the coolest thing Huliona had ever seen. It was a giant mushroom. The mushrooms stem was the top of the dress and the skirt was the cap turned upside down. Huliona got only into her slip then slipped the dress on. She then put the sandals on. The sandals were made completely out of roots that snaked all the way up to Huliona's knees. Huliona stood up and looked in the mirror.

"I love it!" she said. "It's perfect!"

"Oh great!" Colly said.

Then for the next hour and a half the girls tried on their battle armor. Each piece was exquisite and unique, each suited to fit the girl who was wearing it.

Rostoa's armor was a pair of Capri pants and a long short sleeved tunic. Both the pants and the shirt were made out of dark brown bark sewn together roughly to give it a rustic and fierce look. It also had a smooth finish so it shone in the bright light of the fitting room. Rostoa's shoes were flats made out of special dirt found in the western regions of Etarfia.

Cira's armor was a long and flowing yellow and orange dress with spaghetti straps. The dress wrapped around her horizontally at the top until it reached her waist. It then billowed out at her hips into a flowing skirt. It was plain but beautiful. Cira's shoes were made out of fresh sun rays.

Latopa's armor was a dress made out of course silkworm fibers. It was maroon in color and reached her knees. It also had cap sleeves and a v-neck. She had no shoes, but ties in her hair. Her armor was so simple because she would be an animal most of the battle.

Hatara's armor was a pair of shorts and a matching top. Both the shirt and top were made out of turquoise cloud dust, a very rare find. They also had dark blue polka dots and a dark purple trim. Her shoes were very simple, dark purple flats that curled over at the toe.

Clerice's armor was a grey hoop skirt dress. It started at her neck and wrapped around her body until it billowed out into a hoop skirt that reached her knees. It was made from the inside of a tornado. Her shoes were grey boots that reached her knees.

"Thank you Colly." Safferstar said as the girls prepared to leave.

"Ya, thanks Colly."

"You're the best!"

"I love my armor." The girls all chimed in.

"Oh, you're quite welcome!" Colly said. "You are all such a joy! Any time, any time!" she was beaming.

"Hey Colly," Huliona asked. "did you make all our armor?"

"I did."

"Wow! You're so talented! I could have never have done that!" Rostoa said.

Colly blushed. "Why thank you!"

"Well thank you again." Safferstar said. "Come girls, you must really need some rest."

"Yes," Huliona said. "I know I do."

"Dito that." Latopa said yawning. "I'm exhausted!"

"And um," Safferstar muttered quickly. "Katrina has something to tell you later." She turned pail.

"Safferstar are you okay?" Hatara asked. "You look really pail."

"Oh I'm fine! I'm just feeling a bit under the weather at the moment."

"Here, let me take you to the kitchen to get a glass of water." Clerice said. She opened the pine door and proceeded to leave. But just before she left she glanced at the girls, she looked serious. They nodded as she left.

"Wait, how will you find your way back?" Safferstar said, peeking back into the room.

"Oh, we will be okay." Huliona said.

"Well, alright." Safferstar said as she let Clerice lead her down the hall and out of sight.

"Wow, she looked really sick." Latopa said. "I hope she is okay."

"Well she looked pretty pale when Huliona and Hatara fell into the Misting Memory pool." Eliana pointed out. "She wasn't sick then."

"Right," Hulona said. "So I don't think she is under the weather.

"I don't get it." Cira said.

"Well did you notice that she only looked pale when she told us Katrina had to tell us something later?" Huliona said. "I think she only turns pale when something is wrong."

"Oh, ya." Latopa said. "I know what you mean."

"Maybe Katrina has something really important to tell us later." Cira said. "I just hope its not well, bad, or at least not too bad."

"Me too." Huliona said.

"Hey, where's Colly?" Rostoa asked. The girls looked around. Colly was no where to be seen.

"I didn't hear her leave." Eliana said.

Hatara looked uneasy. "Well that's weird." She said. Now all the girls felt uneasy. It had been a strange day. First the sabberon attacking, Safferstar they thought was lying, and now Colly disappears without saying goodbye.

"Come on girls." Latopa said. "We should really get some rest if Katrina has something important to tell us."

The others agreed. They yelled a goodbye to Colly, where ever she was then left the cylinder shaped room.

****

Huliona woke with a start. She had been dreaming that Etarfia had lost the battle and that she had been killed. Huliona shivered as she recalled the dream. She glanced at the clock, twelve thirty. She had only been asleep for a half an hour! Huliona grumbled in irritation as she stumbled out of bed and over to her phone. She rang the kitchens number.

"Hello!" A cheery voice on the other end answered.

"Hi Throrta." Huliona said to the cloud person.

"Hello Queen Huliona, how may I help you?"

"May I please have a glass of water?"

"You sure can! I'll send someone up."

"Oh, Throrta can you send Catton? I wanted to go over the plans we have for the new fountain with him."

"Oh," Throrta said. "To tell you the truth I have not seen him all day."

"Oh, okay. Then anyone will do. Thanks Throrta." Huliona then hung up the phone. She sat down, puzzled. Now that she thought about it she had not seen Catton today either. That was strange because she usually saw Catton all the time. He was either trimming the hedges, sweeping the entrance hall or doing some other chore. She had not seen him doing any of these things.

Huliona left her room. She decided she would check with the others. Huliona wanted to see if they had seen Catton. Huliona walked down the hall a ways until she reached Cira's

The Chronicles of Etarfia

door. She knocked. A few minutes later the door opened and Cira stood there.

"Wow! What happened to you?!" Huliona asked, staring at Cira. Cira had dark brown circles under her eyes, and her hair was a rumpled mess. She looked exhausted.

"Do you remember that spell I told you about?" Cira asked.

"You mean the spell you used to burn a hole in those roots and trees when you were going to save Hatara and me?"

"Yes."

"What about it?'

"Well I was trying to do that spell again. I've been trying and trying but I just can't get it." Cira said.

"Ask Katrina about it. Maybe she knows."

"Maybe. So what's up?"

"Something weird has been happening." Huliona said.

"Come on in." Cira said.

Huliona stepped into Cira's room. Cira's room had a yellow marble floor and yellow walls. The ceiling was a huge skylight to let the sunshine in. Cira's bed, vanity, dresser and side tables were made from hardened sun rays that sparkled. She also had an armchair that was made out of glow worm silk trimmed with gold lace, as were her bed clothes. Around the rest of the room where objects having to do with fire, light and magma. But Huliona's favorite thing in the room was Cira's realistic model of the sun.

The sun sat on a stand about waist high and in the center of the room. The replica was literally a ball of fire and light, it also changed colors for fire is not just yellow and orange, but many different colors such as pink, blue, white, and purple.

Cira flopped down on her rumpled bed. "So what's weird?" She asked.

"Have you seen Catton today?" Huliona asked as she sat in Cira's arm chair.

Cira thought. "Now that you mention it, I have not seen him." She said.

"I haven't either." Huliona said. "And neither has anyone else."

"So?" Cira asked.

"So, I've also had a weird feeling in my gut all day that something is wrong. And I feel as though I'm getting closer to what it is when I found out Catton hasn't been around."

"Me too! But I tried to ignore it. I figured it was nothing."

"Same here. But it just suddenly got really strong."

"So you think the thing that is wrong involves Catton?" Cira said.

"Yes. In fact I'm positive now." Huliona said standing up. "We have to find him."

"Okay." Cira said. "I think you're right. Let's tell the others. Then we can start looking for Catton."

The two girls hurried out of Cira's room. They ran down the hall towards Rostoa's bedroom door. Hopefully she would know what they were talking about.

****

The two Queens finally reached Rostoa's bedroom door. A sign hung on it that read "Beware of attack bear." Ignoring the sign Huliona banged on the heavy oak door. Then what seemed like an eternity later the door opened and a rumpled looking Rostoa stood there.

"Hi." Cira said.

"Hi!" Rostoa said sarcastically, she was still half asleep.

"We have something to tell you." Huliona said, she was getting more nervous by the second.

Rostoa motioned for the girls to follow her into her room. Once inside they told her about Catton not being seen and the weird feeling that something was wrong. Rostoa agreed. She told Cira and Huliona that she had been feeling odd all day as well, and that she also had not seen Catton.

"We should have listened to our gut." Rostoa said as she and the others headed down the hall.

"I know." Huliona said. "From now on we have to listen to our powers."

"I'm annoyed." Cira said.

"Why?" Huliona asked.

"Well the problems never seem to end here." Cira said.

"I know what you mean, but we were sent here to solve these problems." Rostoa said.

"I know I know. It's just so hard."

"It sure is." Huliona said.

Rostoa, Huliona, and Cira left Rostoa's room and told the others about the strange happenings. Every one of them agreed. They knew they had to find Katrina and tell her what was going on.

"Come on!" Hatara yelled as she flew down the hall ahead of her friends. "We have to find Katrina, fast!"

"Easy for you to say!" Latopa called out as she and the others started to run to keep up. "You can fly!"

Soon all seven of them were running down the marble stairs at top speed. Clerice almost fell, but Latopa grabbed her arm just in time. They all reached the bottom of the stair case then ran out in search of Katrina.

Chapter 31

THWONK!

Nathlene dismounted her white horse and looked around for Samrin the stable boy. She soon spotted him.

"Samrin!" Nathlene called. "Come take Floyd to the stable!"

"Yes Nathlene." Samrin said as he took Floyds reins. He led him to the stables.

Nathlene then set about to her task of finding Catton. She saw him pulling up weeds on the edge of the garden. He was putting them in a bucket. Nathlene, nonchalantly, strode over to him.

"Hello Catton." She said.

"Oh, hello Nathlene." Catton said as he stood up, wiping his dirty hands on his pants.

"What are you doing?"

"I'm just pulling up weeds in the garden and planting them some where else. Just like Queen Huliona said."

"Oh, Well I'm here because I noticed that the stable door is coming off its top hinge. Could you fix it?"

"I'll take a look." Catton said as he walked towards the stable. Nathlene smiled as she followed.

The two went inside the stable. Catton looked at the doors. "Which one is it?" He asked.

"The left door." Nathlene said, as she grabbed a garden hoe.

"I don't see anything wrong." Catton said as he examined the hinge closer. He did not see Nathlene coming up behind him.

"Oh, keep looking. Its there." She said.

"No really," Catton said. "there isn't anything wrong." But just as Catton turned around, THWONK! Nathlene hit him in the head with the garden hoe. Catton fell to the ground, unconscious.

"Piece of cake." Nathlene muttered as she threw the garden hoe aside. She then proceeded to grab a brown sack used for the horse's grain and stuff Catton into it.

"Now, for the sabberon." Nathlene said as she dragged the sack out of the stable. She then dragged it behind the stable and into some bushes.

****

Nathlene then slunk back into the castle, knowing that once she freed the sabberon her cover would be blown and she could not return. Trying to push the voice in her head that was telling her this was wrong aside she snuck into the parlor. She ducked behind a pillar as a servant passed.

Nathlene finally made it through the rest of the palace without being caught. Nathlene turned the last corner and faced a very long hallway. She started down it. This hallway was not like the other hallways in the palace at all. It was much danker and dingier. Its walls were covered in dirt and its windows were cracked. The hallway had only one door, the door to the dungeons.

As Nathlene neared the end of the hallway the guards, two tigers, came into view. Once Nathlene saw them she pretended to look worried. She then ran the rest of the way down the hall.

"Oh! Thank goodness I found you!" Nathlene lied as she approached the two guards.

"Yes," The left tiger growled. "What is it?"

"I spotted a sabberon up on Dew Drop Peak." Nathlene said.

"Are you sure?" the right tiger growled. He looked suspicious.

"Yes I'm sure! Now go after it!"

"Who will watch the dungeons?" the left tiger asked.

"I will," Nathlene said. "until you come back."

"Fine." The right guard said after a long pause. "Make sure no one gets in, or out." The two tigers then started off down the hallway.

Nathlene smiled and once they were out of earshot she said. "Oh, but I will be doing quite the opposite." Then once the tigers had turned the corner Nathlene grabbed the ring of keys that were hanging on a hook beside the door. She inserted the first key into the lock and opened the heavy door. It revealed a long narrow stair case descending into the dungeons with oil lit lamps on either side of the stair case to light Nathlene's way.

****

Nathlene stepped onto the first stair and closed the door behind her. She then quickly descended the stairs. At the bottom she found another door. Nathlene took the second key and inserted it into this doors lock. She unlocked this door and entered a very small dimly lit room with a battered table and chairs. It also had an old tapestry on the wall. Nathlene walked through this room and up to the very last door, the door to the prisoner's cells.

Nathlene unlocked this door and walked through. She faced a long hallway with cells on either side. Nathlene cautiously started down the hallway. As she descended down the dark hallway Nathlene would hear evil laughter from one of the witch's creatures or one of them every now and again would call out traitor mockingly.

Nathlene finally reached the end of the hallway; this is where the most secure cell was located. Hands shaking Nathlene inserted the fourth key into the heavy platinum door. Nathlene took a deep breath then turned the key and opened the door.

Nathlene peered into the cell behind the door. There was a large crumpled heap in the left corner. "Sabberon, I have come to release you." Nathlene said.

"Lies." Answered a gruff voice.

"What?"

"All you Etarfian's do is lie!" the sabberon cried out.

"Quiet!" Nathlene said. "And I assure you sabberon, I am not lying."

"Then if you are not lying, answer me this." The sabberon said as he came over to the cell door. "Why would you, of all the people in Etarfia, release me?"

Nathlene sighed and closed her eyes. "It is a long story, but to make it short, I am in line with your masters."

"But, why!?"

"Ugg. Well ever since I said I would be Queen of Etarfia, the very first day I took the job I knew I would someday have to give up my thrown to some, some children. I wasn't too keen on the idea. So just but a few weeks ago, before the Queens arrived I hatched a plan. When the new Queens arrived I would join the other side, no one would expect it, no one would know."

"Good choice." The sabberon said laughter in his words. "For if you had not joined my masters you would have been the first person I would have killed."

Nathlene's face grew pale, she shivered. "Now come," she said as she unlocked the bared door. "We have to get out of here. We are escaping through the west tunnel."

"WE?" The sabberon asked.

"Yes 'we." Nathlene said. "I have a hostage. And besides once they discover you are gone the guards will say I was the only one besides them near the dungeons today. My cover will be blown."

And with that Nathlene and the sabberon started back down the hallway with cells on either side.

****

Once Nathlene and the sabberon reached the top of the dungeon stairs Nathlene unlocked the door and returned the keys to their hook. They then hurried down the hall. Once at the end Nathlene opened a trap door in the worn floor.

"Why in gods name would you put a trap door here?" the sabberon asked.

"It is for emergencies." Nathlene said. "Now come on." Then she and the sabberon climbed down into the hole just as the two tiger guards rounded the corner.

The sabberon bounded ahead of Nathlene through the tunnel. What seemed like hours later to Nathlene they finally reached the end. Nathlene then found the crack in the ceiling that lead out of the tunnel and pushed on it. A door flung open. The sabberon went through first Nathlene followed. They emerged behind the stable.

Nathlene then ran into the stable and grabbed Floyd, she then returned to the back. Nathlene found the sack with Catton in it and slung it over Floyd's back. She then mounted Floyd as well. Then Nathlene and the sabberon took off into the woods, just as it started to rain.

Chapter 32

THE PAIN OF BETRAYLE

Huliona, Cira, Rostoa, Latopa, Clerice, Hatara and Eliana rushed down the stairs as the rain poured down.

"That's weird." Clerice said. "I read the sky, and it wasn't supposed to rain today."

"Something bad must have happened." Hatara said.

As the girls reached the bottom of the staircase Katrina burst in through the door sopping wet and muttering.

"Katrina! We have something to tell you!" Latopa said running ahead of the others.

"I have something to tell you too."

"Us first." Huliona said.

"Okay, shoot."

"Have you seen Catton today?" Cira asked.

"That's what you wanted to say?"

"Just answer the question." Eliana said.

Katrina thought, "Now that you mention it, I have not seen him."

"We haven't seen him either." Huliona said. "We have also had the feeling that something is wrong, all day."

"Really? Well why didn't you tell me sooner?" Katrina said looking a bit annoyed.

"We um," Huliona said meekly. "We ignored it."

"You ignored it!" Katrina bellowed.

"We figured it was nothing!" Eliana said jumping to Huliona's defense.

"Alright, alright." Katrina said. "I will go find Nathlene. Wait here." Katrina then hurried from the room.

She returned about ten minutes later looking confused and frustrated. "Nathlene is not here." Katrina said.

"What do you mean she's not here?" Rostoa said.

"I went to her room and she wasn't there, I went to the dinning room and parlor. I even asked a few servants about her. They told me they had not seen her since the sabberon attacked this morning."

"This is getting really weird." Latopa said.

"Wait! Samrin the stable boy might know." Clerice said. "Nathlene never goes on a journey without her horse, Samrin will know if she went anywhere today."

"Oh good work Clerice!" Katrina said, as she ran into the kitchen where Samrin was drying off from the rain.

"Samrin," Katrina said approaching him. "Did Nathlene go anywhere today?"

"Yes," Samrin said thinking. "I believe she did."

"Do you know where she went?"

"No. l only saw her when she came back, and when she did I took Floyd to the stable. When I came out of the stable she was talking to Catton."

"You saw Catton!" Katrina blurted out.

"Yes. Nathlene seemed to have told him something. They both went into the stable. Then I left."

"Thank you Samrin!" Katrina said. She then hurried back to the girls.

"What did he say?" Huliona asked.

"I'll tell you on the way to the stable." Katrina answered.

Confused but willing to follow, the girls grabbed their cloaks and followed Katrina out into the rain. Eliana twirled in the rain as Katrina told them what Samrin had said.

"So you think they are in the stables?" Latopa asked.

"No, but there may be evidence of why they went there." Katrina said.

"You think they are together?" Rostoa asked.

"Yes." Katrina answered.

They all finally reached the stables. Clerice pulled the heavy door open and everyone stepped inside. The moment Katrina stepped into the stables she knew that the worst had happened. As she stared at the ground, something knotted in her stomach.

"What is it?" Cira asked, she then fell silent and stared. The others looked.

Right in front of Katrina was an imprint of a mushroom boy in the dirt. A garden hoe lay near by, and there were high-heel marks everywhere.

"What is it?" Huliona repeated sadly. "Nathlene has betrayed us."

****

Katrina staggered and felt nauseous. Could one of the old Queens of Etarfia, Katrina's Nathlene, be a traitor? She started to black out. Rostoa ran to her and caught her before she hit the ground.

"Oh my gosh! Are you okay?" Eliana cried as she ran to help Rostoa.

"I'm fine." Katrina said righting herself. "But I understand now, why Nathlene has been acting mean, not talking to me, being secretive."

"Katrina, I think we should get you back to the palace." Hatara said. "You don't look too good."

"No, no I'm fine."

"It looks as if he's been dragged." Cira said, inspecting the floor. "Over here. Look at all these marks in the sand."

"There used to be two grain sacks over there, now there's only one." Clerice trailed off.

Katrina fell again and Rostoa caught her. "I know what she did." Katrina said, now sad and confused. "Right after the sabberon attacked, she went to the evil witch's castle. They probably told her to get them a captive and what ever else they wanted. So when she got back to the palace she lied to Catton about something in the stables to get him in here. Then she knocked him out, and took him."Katrina was paler than before. "She put him in a grain sack and probably went to..." Katrina trailed off.

"THE SABBERON!" Everyone yelled.

"Okay, Huliona, Hatara, go follow Nathlene. Eliana, Latopa, and Cira go see if the sabberon is still in his cell. Clerice and I will take Katrina inside and find Safferstar." Rostoa said.

"No!" Katrina said.

"What?" Latopa said.

"I am going after Nathlene." Katrina said. "It has to be me."

"But you can't go alone." Latopa said. "What if the sabberon really is free? He could hurt you."

"I'll be fine. I know how to handle the sabberon. I've been fighting him for years." Katrina said as she saddled her horse Sophia. "Find Safferstar and go see if the sabberon has escaped. Do not come after me, ya hear?"

The girls nodded reluctantly. Then Katrina jumped onto Sophia and rode out into the rain.

****

The seven Queens and Safferstar hurried through the palace. Multiple servants asked what was wrong, but they ignored them and pushed past, too worried to answer. Finally they reached the dingy hall way that led to the dungeons. They all sprinted down it.

Once they reached the end Latopa addressed the tiger guards. "Please move aside."

"What business do you have in the dungeons?" the right tiger guard asked.

"I said move aside!!" Latopa yelled with surprising ferocity. "I am Queen and I should be able to get into the dungeons when I want to! I'm sorry but this is urgent!"

The tiger guards looking taken aback moved aside. Cira grabbed the ring of keys and quickly unlocked the door. They all raced down the stairs as the tiger guards stared after them, wondering what was wrong.

"Latopa," Huliona said. "I didn't know you could do that!"

"Well, a desperate time calls for desperate measures. I don't normally talk to them like that." Latopa looked a little guilty.

"It's alright." Safferstar said. "We had to get down here as quickly as possible."

"I just hope our trip isn't wasted." Hatara said as they reached the end of the stairs.

Cira unlocked the second door. All of them entered the small room with the battered table and chairs that Nathlene had walked through only hours before.

Finally they reached the last door. Cira unlocked it and they entered the room only to hear shouts of anger and hatred from all the prisoners.

"You better shut up! Or I will keep you all locked in these dungeons for eternity!" Safferstar bellowed at the top of her lungs. Most of the prisoners ignored the small sprite kin.

The girls sped down the hall of cells until they came to the very end where the heavy platinum door stood. "Cross your fingers girls." Cira said as she inserted the last key.

Huliona was the first to peer into the cell behind the door. She saw a large irregular lump in the left corner. "Cira, give me the keys." She said. Cira handed Huliona the keys. Huliona unlocked the cell door and went in, they others followed wearily behind.

They all approached the lump. But once they were close enough they noticed that the lump was not the sabberon, but bails of hay, piled on top of each other.

****

Katrina ran Sophia hard through the forest, pine branches whipping her in the face, not having time to move. But when Katrina came out onto the dirt road she slowed down.

She almost stopped altogether believing she would never catch up to Nathlene. Katrina almost turned around to go back to the palace and find another way to rescue Catton. But she didn't. For just at that moment up ahead Nathlene rode out of the woods. She was riding fast and to Katrina's dismay, a brown sack was slung over Floyds back. Then Katrina's heart skipped a beat, the sabberon ran out of the woods next and started to run beside Nathlene.

"No..." Katrina whispered. She couldn't believe it. The woman who had found her on the beach as a baby and raised her, and was even the Queen of Etarfia, was a traitor?

Katrina stayed well behind Nathlene for the whole ride, but kept her in sight, and all the while she resisted the urge, to cry.

****

What seemed like an hour later Nathlene stopped in front of a high stone wall with a gate built into the front. Nathlene slipped of off Floyd. Katrina knew this would be her only chance to rescue Catton. So she mustered up all of her courage and rode out into the open.

Katrina startled the sabberon and Nathlene as she rode toward them. The sabberon jumped up onto the wall. Nathlene screamed and banged her head on one of the stones. Katrina ran up to Floyd and grabbed his reins. She then circled around him and sped back the way she had come.

Katrina looked back for a split second. She saw the sabberon smile wickedly and jump off the wall onto the other side. She then saw Nathlene, who looked stunned and heartbroken.

****

"How dare she!!!" Hatara screamed. The scream was so loud that the creatures in to cells quieted.

"I, I, I could just wring her neck!!" Latopa shouted.

"Well now we know for sure she is a traitor!" Rostoa said angrily.

"She must have waited until we were getting fitted for our battle armor; there is no other time she could have done it." Huliona said.

"Well do the guards know?" Clerice asked, exasperated.

"They must not." Cira said. "I doubt they would have let Nathlene in if they knew what she was up too."

"Well, let's go ask them." Eliana said.

****

Everyone hurried to the dungeon stairs.

"You know," Latopa said. "Huliona and I were suspicious of Nathlene when we first arrived."

"I just wish we listened to our powers sooner." Huliona said.

Everyone finally reached the top of the stairs and burst out into the hallway.

"The sabberon is gone!" Safferstar yelled at the tiger guards, who now looked a little frightened.

"Impossible." The right tiger guard said.

"I assure you the sabberon is gone. And we think Nathlene is behind it." Safferstar said.

"Nathlene!" The left tiger guard scoffed. "I highly doubt it."

"Was Nathlene here today?" Safferstar asked.

The tigers said nothing.

"Answer me!"

"Yes. She told us she had spotted a sabberon up on Dew Drop Peak. So we went to check it out. When we came back she was gone."

"Well there is your proof!" Safferstar said.

Then all eight girls left the dingy hallway.

****

Katrina rode far away from Nathlene, and the rain kept on falling. The ride back to the palace did not seem as long as the ride away. Maybe it was because the deed was done, Katrina didn't know. She didn't care; she was too heartbroken to care.

Katrina finally reached the palace. When she did she led Floyd and Sophia into the stable. Once inside Katrina took the brown sack and put it on the ground. She pulled it open; Catton was inside with a big lump on his head.

"Still unconscious." She muttered. "Nathlene must have knocked you out pretty good."

Katrina picked up Catton and hoisted him over her shoulder. She then left the stable and strode across the palace yard, the rain pouring down, soaking her to the skin. It seemed as if Etarfia itself was crying.

****

"Katrina!!" The girls cried as she came through the huge double doors.

Katrina laid Catton down in front of them. "Catton!" Huliona cried as she ran towards him, the others following. They all circled him.

"Is he okay?" Rostoa asked.

"He looks dead to me." Eliana said.

"He's not dead!" Huliona said feeling his wrist for a pulse. "He was just knocked out."

"Was he with Nathlene?" Latopa asked.

"Yes," Katrina said tight lipped. Then as if her heart just burst open she collapsed to the floor crying "My life is a lie!"

Safferstar knelt down beside Katrina and put her hand on her shoulder. "I think we all feel that way right now." She said sadly.

"I just can't believe it. All those years, I, I thought she cared!" Katrina cried.

"Maybe she did." Safferstar said. Katrina looked up. "This was her decision Katrina; it had nothing to do with you."

"Maybe, but I will not accept the fact that she lied to me." A tear rolled down Katrina's cheek.

The girls were surprised. They never thought they would see Katrina cry, as tough as she was.

"I'm going to go lay down." Katrina said. She then took one last look at the girls and retreated to her room.

"Huliona, since you are Catton's Queen he will rest in your room. Look after him."

"Okay." Huliona said.

****

Huliona grabbed Catton's legs and Eliana grabbed his arms, they hoisted him up the stairs. They dragged him down the hall and into Huliona's room. Clerice put a bamboo mat down on the floor; the girls then put Catton on it. Latopa then threw a blanket over him.

"Cool room!" Hatara said flopping down on Huliona's bed. "Thanks."

Cira gawked at the canopy ceiling.

"It needs more stone." Rostoa said looking around.

"Of course you would say that!" Latopa said with a laugh.

They all were silent. "I'm glad he's okay." Clerice finally said, gesturing to Catton.

"Me too." Huliona said.

"But I don't get why Nathlene would go and turn on us. It doesn't make any sense." Eliana said.

"Maybe it's because we took her job." Hatara pointed out.

Latopa placed a blanket over him, and put a pillow under his head.

The others agreed. Then talk moved on to other things, as the rain turned into a light drizzle.

Chapter 33

BAD NEWS

The next day was quiet. It had stopped raining, to Eliana's dismay, and was now damp and humid outside. It was the kind of weather no one, except for Clerice, wanted to go out in.

Of course, Nathlene had not come back that night. But just in case the girls planned to lock her in the dungeons forever. Rostoa thought they should banish Nathlene from Etarfia altogether and get rid of her. They were all furious and sad.

Katrina had stayed in her room the whole night. She had not come down for supper or breakfast. Cira was even sent up to listen at her door, but when she came back Cira reported Katrina was silent. The girls knew that Nathlene betraying them had affected her greatly.

****

"I'm bored." Huliona announced as she slumped onto the parlor couch. She looked at the others.

Latopa had turned into a bob cat and was asleep on the floor. Cira was making a fire crystal, which in fact was very hard to do. Clerice was gazing out the window. Rostoa was reading "Into the Mountains" which Safferstar had been able to get for her. Hatara was trying to make a stair case of air only she could walk on. Eliana was making water spheres, freezing them, and stacking them into pyramids.

"Hmmm?" Rostoa said glancing up from her book.

"I'm bored." Huliona repeated.

"Me too." Rostoa said putting her book aside. "I mean I love this book and all, but I've read it almost nine times. It gets kinda boring."

Huliona nodded in agreement but she looked troubled.

"Is something wrong?" Rostoa asked.

"I'm kind of getting worried about Katrina." Huliona confessed.

"I am too." Rostoa said.

"She must be really hungry." Eliana put in. "She didn't come down for supper or breakfast."

"That is a sign that she's really upset." Rostoa said.

"I think we should go and talk to her." Cira said looking up from her fire crystal. "She's been awfully quiet."

"Oh NO! No, no, no, no! That is a very bad idea." Huliona said.

"Why?"

"Because," Eliana answered. "she is angry and sad. She would defiantly not want us up there."

"Hmph!" Cira said, sticking her nose in the air.

"Oh stop being so stubborn!" Hatara said finishing another stair. "Eliana and Huliona are right. Katrina would not want us barging in on her."

"What I want to know is what she wants to tell us." Clerice said coming over to the others.

"Oh me too!" Hatara said. "I'm itching to know!"

Huliona sighed. "I guess she will tell us when she is ready."

Than at that moment Catton walked in. "Catton!" All the girls cried and rushed over to him. Shortly after Catton had been taken to Huliona's room, someone had come and taken him to Belrane. So they had not seen him for a while.

"Are you feeling better?" Huliona asked.

"A little." Catton answered.

"It must have been so traumatic!" Cira said.

"You know I don't really remember any of it." Catton admitted.

Latopa had woken up and turned back into her human form. She walked over to the others. "How's your head?" She asked sleepily.

"It hurts a lot." Catton answered. Catton motioned to the big bruise on his head.

"That's a BIG bruise." Hatara exclaimed, staring.

"Well the reason I am here is Katrina has called for you." Catton said.

"Katrina!" The girls cried. They all ran from the room, nearly trampling Catton.

The girls ran up the marble staircase and down the hall. They ran the very end where a set of double doors stood, Katrina's bedroom doors.

Rostoa knocked. "Come in." A meek voice answered. Rostoa opened the door and they all filed in.

The girls gasped. Katrina was a sight to see. She had dark circles under her eyes, her hair was a rumpled mess, she had not changed from the day before and she was sitting on the floor.

"Come sit." Katrina said.

The girls approached Katrina and sat down in a circle around her. "I have something to tell you." Katrina started. The girls nodded, uneasy and wide eyed. "Now you must know that what I am about to tell you was not my decision." The girls nodded. Katrina took a deep breath, "The battle is in two days."

"Excuse me, what?" Rostoa said.

"The battle is in two days." Katrina repeated, bracing for panic.

"Okay," Clerice said getting tense.

"No!" Hatara yelled, jumping to her feet. "How could you do this to us? We are hardly ready," Hatara looked wildly around the room. "We are going to get killed! We're doomed!"

"This was not my decision."

"Then who's decision was it?! Clover's?! We'll be lucky if only one of us survives!" Hatara charged from the room.

"Hatara!" Eliana yelled. Everyone jumped up and ran from the room. Latopa was the only one to look back, and she saw Katrina still sitting on the floor, sad eyed.

Hatara made it down the hall and the stairs, but that was as far as she got before she collapsed.

"Hatara!" Huliona yelled. Reaching her first Huliona grabbed Hatara's shoulders and helped her up.

"Hatara, listen to me, everything is going to be alright." Huliona said.

Hatara shook her head no.

"No! It is." Huliona said. "Do you think Safferstar would have come for us if she knew we could not defeat these witches? Do you think she would put seven girls into battle if she knew they would fail?"

"No." Hatara squeaked.

"No she wouldn't have. So are you going to flee when these people need our help?"

"No." Hatara said. "I, I just got so afraid."

"It's okay." Cira said.

"Ya, we all get afraid." Rostoa added.

"So, I guess we know what we are doing today." Latopa said.

"Battle plans." Clerice and Eliana said together.

****

Nathlene yelped in pain as she was thrown across the floor. She stared at Capsa in fear. "You fool! How could you have gotten caught!?" Capsa raged, green static electricity flying from her hands, her eyes gleaming with anger.

"I, I didn't know anyone was watching." Nathlene pleaded rising to her knees. "I looked around before I even took Catton!" Nathlene cowered as Capsa advanced.

"So Samrin, the stable boy, doesn't count as someone?" Capsa hissed. "You ALWAYS make sure no one even sees you when you do a deed like this!" Capsa hit Nathlene with more electricity. Nathlene cried out and grabbed her leg. Then Dase entered the room. Nathlene now terrified backed against the wall, anticipating another blow.

"I, have heard about Nathlene's, little blunder." She said quietly.

"So what should we do with her?" Capsa asked.

"We could give her back to the Etarfian's." Dase said. "Oh wouldn't they be pleased." she laughed.

"I have a better idea." Capsa said. "Let's throw her into the dungeons, and torture her every day. For the rest of her miserable pathetic life."

"Good idea." Dase laughed wickedly.

"No, no! You can't do this! It was my choice to join you!" Nathlene cried desperately.

"Exactly!" Dase cried. "Which means you are on our side now, and there for belong to us."

Capsa then snapped her fingers, the sound echoed throughout the castle. The sabberon entered the room.

"No!" Nathlene cried.

The sabberon smiled, displaying his sharp teeth. He grabbed Nathlene in his mouth. But he bit down a little harder than he should have. He did not wound Nathlene but he did give her a bruise to remember.

"No! PLEASE!! STOP!" Nathlene's cries echoed down the dingy hallway.

"Now that that idiot is out of the way we can focus on more important matters." Capsa said.

"Like getting those wrenched kids out of the way!" Dase said.

"Where do we start?" Capsa asked.

****

The seven Queens of Etarfia hurried down the hallway to Colly's studio.

"I hope she is there." Eliana said.

"I'm sure she will be." Cira said as they approached Colly's door. "Where would she have to go?"

Hatara grabbed the handle and pushed the door open. The girls all filed in. They immediately noticed how quiet the room was. It was almost eerie; no sound what so ever could be heard.

"Colly!" Huliona called. "Colly, we are here to pick up our armor. Are the alterations finished?" There was no answer.

"Colly?" Rostoa called out. Suddenly there was a noise from the back room. The girls turned toward it. The door opened and Colly came out warily.

"Hi Colly, we are here to…" But that was all Clerice got out before Colly shushed her.

"Please my Queens, will you keep it down?" She asked.

The girls, confused, nodded. "Now, what is it you want?" Colly asked.

"We have come to pick up our armor." Eliana whispered. "Is it ready?"

Colly nodded and ran back into the back room. She returned with seven bags. She gave each girl her armor. "There you are, now run along." Colly said. She looked uncomfortable.

"Colly, are you alright?" Latopa asked. "You're acting a bit, strange."

"Oh, I'm fine, perfectly fine. Now go." Colly tried to usher them to the door.

"Are you sure?" Huliona asked.

"Yes, yes I'm sure." Colly said. She smiled reassuringly.

"Well okay." The girls turned to leave.

"But Huliona," Colly said. Huliona turned back and Colly pulled her right up to her face. "There, is some thing not right today." She whispered. "Not everything is in balance. Danger lurks." Colly looked at Huliona. "Just do me a favor, don't go outside." Colly then turned to the others. She looked at them for a minute then turned and ran back into the back room. Colly shut the door and bolted it.

The girls stared after her, all of them were confused. "What did she say?" Cira asked.

"She said there was danger and to not go outside." Huliona answered.

"Well that's weird." Latopa said frowning.

"She must have gone off the deep end." Rostoa mumbled.

Hatara shot her a look. "Come on guys." She said. "Let's go see what's outside."

****

The girls left Colly's studio and dropped their armor off at their rooms. They all then met in the entry hall.

"There could be nothing outside." Cira said nervously. "Maybe Colly was joking."

"She didn't sound like she was joking when she told me." Huliona said. "She sounded worried."

"Besides," Eliana said. "Why would she joke about something like that? That's kinda mean if you ask me."

"Eliana's right." Latopa said her hand on the door handle. "Let's just go see." Latopa then pushed open the door.

A heavy fog had settled over the castle yard and the lake. Everyone then realized their situation. They were in a thick fog and couldn't see, and if there really was any danger, they were in big trouble.

"I'll take care of it." Clerice said. Clerice held up her arms and put her hands together. She the slowly parted her hands, as she did this a path formed in the fog.

"Good work Clerice!" Rostoa said as all seven of them headed down the path.

As they headed down the path the girls looked about them warily. They knew Colly was right, for now they felt a pit in their stomachs and a chill creeping up their spine. They all stopped in the middle of the path. They all felt like the pray on a hunt. A twig cracked. All the girls whirled around.

"Guys," Latopa stammered. "something is moving over there." Latopa pointed into the fog where a black shape was stealthily moving along the tree line.

Clerice turned to move the fog out of the way. "No," Huliona whispered, grasping Clerice's hands. "If you move the fog then whatever that is will know we see it."

The girls, unsure of what to do waited. A minute passed, then suddenly without warning a huge black creature jumped out of the fog. Hatara screamed as the creature pinned down Eliana. It bit into her arm, deep. Eliana cried out in pain. She then turned on the creature. She blasted water into its eyes, and then froze it so the creature couldn't see.

"What is that thing!?" Hatara yelled.

"I don't know!" Rostoa shouted back.

Hatara flew into the air above the creature. She sucked all the oxygen away from it so it couldn't breathe. The creature grabbed its throat and wailed. It was one of the most hideous sounds any of the girls had ever heard. Huliona then threw her hands onto the ground. The ground shook and four huge mushrooms sprouted where the creature was standing. They wrapped around its ankles and held it down. Rostoa then turned her arm into a stone arm and hit the creature over the head. The creature went limp instantly.

Cira then ran up to the creature, magma spewed from her hands. She made a dome like enclosure around it and left the front open. Clerice then shot thick bolts of lightning from her hands. They settled into the open space at the front of the dome to make a barrier.

Meanwhile Latopa had turned into a snake and curled tightly around Eliana's arm, so the bleeding would stop.

****

"Hatara, go get Safferstar." Huliona said. The girls were all leaning over Eliana who was moaning with pain. Hatara lifted into the sky and flew away from the concerned group into the palace.

"Eliana!? Eliana can you hear me?" Rostoa asked.

"The pain. The pain is too much!" Eliana wheezed turning to Rostoa.

"It will be okay. Hatara has gone to get Safferstar. This will all be over before you know it." Rostoa said.

"Latopa, has the blood clotted?" Cira asked.

"Yes. She will not loose anymore blood." Latopa said.

Suddenly the palace doors burst open and Safferstar charged across the palace yard with nine rock guards following.

"What happened?!" she cried as she knelt down beside Eliana.

"Some, thing, attacked us!" Clerice said.

"But we took care of it." Huliona said pointing to the dome of hardened magma.

Safferstar walked over to the dome and peered through the lightning bars at the front. Her lips tightened. She put her hand to her forehead.

"What is it?" Cira asked coming over.

"It is a shape shifter." Safferstar answered looking up.

"A shape shifter?" Latopa said looking confused.

"It is like you Latopa, only not nearly as powerful." Safferstar explained. "It is in it's true form right now. It looks like a dragon only smaller and without wings. Its skin is also black and flabby."

Rostoa walked up to the dome and scrunched up her nose. "That thing is really gross!" she said.

Safferstar turned back to the rock guards. "You two scout the woods, you three, scout the palace grounds, and you three, get Queen Eliana inside, call for Esha, she is a healer. You Sidiouse," Safferstar turned to the last rock guard. "Tripple the guards everywhere, this attack was not a mistake."

****

Eliana was lying in bed. Latopa still wrapped around her arm and the others still crowded around her, they would not leave her side for a minute. At least fifteen guards were patrolling the bedroom. Most of them were water sharillons and ice wolves. There were five other guards outside Eliana's door.

Safferstar had gone with the rock guards to fetch Esha. She was the unicorn that the girls had saved from the sabberon; many said she was a fantastic healer.

"Are you feeling better?" Clerice asked.

"Not much." Eliana said.

"You will soon." Latopa said. "Safferstar has gone to get a healer."

Eliana closed her eyes and sighed. "I thank you guys from the bottom of my heart for saving me." She said.

"Oh, don't mention it." Rostoa said. "We know you would do the same for us."

Eliana smiled. A moment later the door opened and Safferstar came in followed by Esha.

"She is over there." Safferstar said pointing to the cluster of girls.

"Greetings my Queens." Esha said as she approached them.

"Hello Esha." Everyone said.

"Thank you so much for coming." Huliona said.

"Oh, anything for my Queens!" Esha replied. The girls then moved aside so Esha could examine Eliana.

"How are you feeling Queen Eliana?" Esha asked, leaning in.

"Faint." Eliana replied in a whisper.

"Queen Latopa, you did the right thing, curling up around the wound. You may have saved Queen Eliana's life." Esha said.

Latopa smiled.

"May I see the wound?"

Latopa uncurled from around Eliana's arm and slithered to the floor. She then changed back into her human form. She was stiff and her clothes were very rumpled.

Esha inspected the wound. She then turned to Safferstar. "I need a wet cloth, sea water, a bowl of sea foam and a seaweed hide bandage." She instructed. Safferstar nodded then sent one of the water sharillons to get the things.

Once the water sharillon returned Esha got to work. "Now," she said. "I have found a tooth in the wound. I'm going to have to remove it. It may hurt a little."

Eliana nodded.

Esha bent her head down and touched the tip of her horn to the wound. Suddenly shimmers of sparkles and lights showered from her horn. Then a tooth started to work its way out of the wound. Eliana clenched her teeth but kept silent. She was strong.

The girls gasped as the tooth was fully taken out. "That was the main problem." Esha told them. "Shape shifter teeth are covered in poison."

"It's so big." Huliona gasped staring at the tooth.

"We should defiantly dispose of it." Safferstar said. "It is still poisonous."

"I'll do it." Cira offered. Cira reached up and picked the tooth out of the air. She then closed it up in her fist. Cira then ignited her hand in flame. A minute later she put the fire out and opened her hand, the tooth was ashes.

"Does it hurt when you do that?" Latopa asked, curious.

"No." Cira said. "It doesn't really feel any different from normal." Cira then went to the window and threw the ashes into the breeze.

Esha then cleaned to wound. She spread the sea foam on the gash then wrapped it tightly with the seaweed hide. "This will heal in about an hour." She said.

"Just an hour?" Rostoa asked, surprised. "It looks like that would take weeks to heal."

"Here in Etarfia wounds do not take as long to heal as they do in your world." Esha told the girls.

"Neat!" Hatara exclaimed.

"Girls I want you to go to your rooms. You need to be as safe as possible." Safferstar said.

"No Safferstar. We want to stay with Eliana until she is well." Huliona said.

Safferstar gave the girls a pleading look. But they stood their ground. "Well, okay." She said hesitantly. "But you are not allowed to leave this room."

The girls nodded. Safferstar then left the room with Esha. The girls either sat on either side of Eliana's huge bed or on the floor.

"How are you feeling now?" Hatara asked.

"Much better." Eliana answered with a laugh.

The girls looked up. The door was opening. "How's it going?" Katrina asked.

****

"Katrina!" the girls cried.

Katrina walked over the where Eliana lay." Are you okay? I was so worried!"

"Yes, I'm fine." Eliana said.

"So a shape shifter attacked you huh?" Katrina said. "Were you scared?"

"Well not..." Huliona started to say but Latopa suddenly burst out.

"It was amazing!"

"It was!" Cira added. "When it had a hold of Eliana's arm she blasted its eyes with water then froze it!"

"You should have seen how mad it was!" Rostoa said. "Then after that Hatara sucked all of its oxygen away so it couldn't breath!"

"Then Huliona trapped it by wrapping mushrooms around its legs!" Clerice exclaimed.

"Then Rostoa knocked it out!" Huliona cried.

"After that Cira made a magma dome around it, imprisoning him!!" Hatara said.

"Then Clerice put a barrier of lightning in the front of the dome!" Latopa cried.

"But Latopa was the best," Cira said. "She turned into a snake and wrapped around Eliana's arm to stop the wound from bleeding."

"Yah, you're a true hero Latopa!" Huliona said. Everyone cheered in agreement. Latopa turned red and smiled.

"It sounds like all you girls are true heroes!" Katrina said. "I'm so proud of you! You have really progressed in you powers since you got here!" Katrina finished excitement and joy shining in her eyes for the first time in days.

"We learned from the best!" Huliona said.

"You sure did!" Katrina said. All the girls laughed. The old Katrina was back. "Now let's go, your soul mates are waiting."

"Go where?" Rostoa asked.

"To the conference room of course! We have to plan out the battle."

"But Safferstar said that we were not to leave this room." Latopa said.

Katrina smirked, "What Safferstar doesn't know will not hurt her. Besides, it's getting late and we must start planning the army's formation and how we will attack."

The girls were silent for a moment. "Well, okay." Clerice said.

"Alright let's go!" Katrina said. "Eliana, do you feel okay to walk?"

Eliana sat up slowly and swung her legs over the side of the bed, then stood up. "Oh ya, I'll be okay. I actually felt worse lying down."

The girls then left the room, to the guards protest. "Where are the guards that were out here?" Huliona asked looking up and down the hall.

"I sent them off." Katrina replied. "I told them I would watch you."

The girls then started off down the hallway. Once they reached the marble stairs they started down them like they had a hundred times before. When they reached the bottom they saw their soul mates waiting. Melark, Eliana's ice wolf worry clearly spread across her face bounded towards Eliana. "My Queen!" She cried "are you alright? I was so worried!"

"I'm fine Melark." Eliana said. "Thank you."

"Where is that blasted shape shifter! I will tear it to pieces!" Melark growled.

"The shape shifter has been taken to the Lu Lu Twin Guard in the Sky for questioning." Katrina answered.

The worry and anger in Melark's face disappeared and she relaxed. "Good," She said. "he will be taken care of there."

"Come," Yotru, Cira's phoenix said. "We mustn't be seen in the halls."

"Yes, Yotru is right." Katrina said. "Follow me."

The conference room was bigger than the girls had expected. The room was a little smaller then their bedrooms, which were pretty big. All four walls were lined with book shelves which reached the cathedral ceiling. Books were crammed into every one.

"Oh, cool!" Eliana exclaimed grabbing a book off the nearest shelf. "World war two." Eliana flipped through the books pages. "I thought since you became a magical realm you didn't have this type of stuff."

"Oh we do." Katrina said. "All these books have to do with war. We use them for reference."

Clerice glanced over at Rostoa who was staring up at the ceiling looking astounded. Clerice followed her gaze and her jaw dropped. "Whoa!" she exclaimed.

The others looked up as well. Cries of surprise rang out from all of them as they noticed what was on the ceiling. On the ceiling were life size paintings of each of them, battle armor and everything. Who ever had painted them had gotten everything perfect, down to the last freckle.

"That, that's amazing!" Huliona exclaimed.

"Who painted it?" Latopa asked. "It looks exactly like us."

"I can't remember her name." Katrina admitted. "But I do know she was a great she wizard. She was mysterious and wise. People said she knew a lot we didn't know. She never talked. She also left the very second she finished."

"How did she know what we look like?" Hatara asked.

"I'm not sure." Katrina said, staring at the ceiling. "She just, knew."

Hatara flew up to the ceiling and touched her delicately painted face. She felt a small surge of magic tickle her finger tips. Goose bumps arose on her arms.

"Come we must get started." Katrina said. "We can't lose anymore time."

Hatara flew back down to the others. "I think we should start on the air battle formations." Cira said.

"Good idea." said Huliona. And so they started, scratching plans, making new ones. They wanted everything to be perfect; they worked late into the night.

Chapter 34

DAWN

Clerice opened her eyes. Light streamed in from her open window. She stretched and smiled.

"What glorious weather! As there is every day!" She announced to herself. Clerice then jumped out of her puffy grey cloud bed. She walked across her static floor. Clerice grabbed her bathrobe and put it on. She then left her room and skipped down the hall to Cira's.

Clerice peeked into Cira's bedroom. She then quietly slipped in. Clerice glided across the floor and over to Cira's bed. Clerice then started shaking Cira.

"Cira! Cira, wake up!" she cried.

Cira groaned.

"Cira! Look at the weather!" Cleric e cried, hoping that would get her out of bed.

Cira took her head out of her pillow and looked up at her skylight. "The sun." she said smiling. Cira then stuffed her face back into her pillow and pulled the covers up over her head.

"Cira!" Clerice pleaded. Clerice then grabbed Cira's covers and threw them on the floor.

"Ahh!" Cira curled up into a ball; her yellow pajamas making her look like an egg yoke.

"It's the dawn of battle!" Clerice cried.

Cira sat up. "The battles happening!" she cried jumping out of bed.

Clerice laughed. "No!" she said.

Cira frowned. "But you said it was the dawn of battle."

"I meant it was very close to the battle." Clerice exclaimed.

"Ya," Cira said. "It really is." She said, looking thoughtful.

Clerice nodded, looking solemn. "No turning back now."

They girls were silent for a moment. "Are you hungry?" Clerice suddenly asked.

Cira paused. A loud rumbling sound filled the room. "Yup!" she said slipping on her orange slippers and rubbing her stomach.

"Me too!" Clerice exclaimed. "but I'm like REALLY hungry. More than I've ever been before."

"Me too. That's weird." Cira said. "I remember us both feeling stuffed after dinner."

"So do I." Clerice agreed. "Let's go get something to eat."

The two young Queens left Cira's room and started down the hall. They soon encountered Hatara.

"Hi guys." Hatara said as she walked over.

"Hi Hatara." Clerice said.

"Are you really hungry?" Cira asked.

Hatara paused, looking confused. She tilted her head towards the ceiling. "Wait, yes, yes I am." she exclaimed.

"So are we!" Cira said.

Hatara laughed. "Well it is morning and we do need to eat breakfast."

"No! It's an unusual kind of hunger!" Clerice said. "I mean REALLY hungry, like we haven't eaten in weeks."

"Ya, I guess your right." Hatara said. "Suddenly I just got this rush of hunger. Oh! I bet it's all linked! I bet everyone is hungry."

The girls all agreed. They then proceeded down the hallway once more, heading for the kitchen. Suddenly Rostoa's bedroom door flew open, knocking Hatara down.

"I need food!" Rostoa shouted into the hallway. Rostoa then peeked around her door. "Oh, hi guys."

"Hi!" Hatara mumbled, sarcastically as she got up off the floor. I feel like I haven't eaten in years!" Rostoa said. She then glanced at the moss carpet. "That dirt looks really good!" She said, smirking. Rostoa then walked over the moss runway carpet. She pulled up an edge and grabbed a handful of dirt from underneath.

"No!" Hatara cried running to Rostoa and prying the dirt from her hand. Although, it did look pretty appetizing.

Cira laughed out loud. She then started down the hall once more, now even hungrier.

"Come on!" Hatara said as she dragged Rostoa down the hall. "We are almost to the kitchen."

"No we're not." Rostoa said.

The four finally reached the stairs. "You know, I don't feel like walking." Clerice said. Clerice then started rubbing her fingers together. Soon sparks of lightning were licking them hungrily. Clerice sprinkled a few on the top step of the stairs. Suddenly two long rods of lightning descended the stairs; smaller rods connected the two larger ones forming a slide.

Clerice then went to jump on, but before she could someone flew past her. "Weeeee!!" Huliona a cried as she sped down the slid on her stomach.

"Hey!" Clerice called after her laughing. "No fair!"

Next came Eliana who sprayed water on the slide to make herself go faster. She flew down the slide. There was a huge splash at the end and a collection of giggles. Then Latopa jumped onto the slide turning into a seal mid air. There was another huge splash and even more laughter from below.

"Okay!" Clerice said. "I am defiantly going next!" Clerice jumped onto the slide. Cira went next the Hatara and Rostoa. They all made huge splashes. By the end they were all in hysterics for they were all sopping wet. Eliana then sucked the water back into her hands and Clerice sucked the lightning back into hers. Hatara then air dried them all.

Then rowdy and rambunctious all seven starving Queens rampaged into the kitchen. "Do you have any food?" Huliona asked as they all made their grand entrance.

Throrta looked up from sweeping and Catton looked up from washing the dishes. Throrta laughed. "Why, of course!"

Cira immediately started to raid the snack drawer. She found many bags of sunflower seeds. She then proceeded to shovel them into her mouth. Hatara had started on the donuts and Latopa on dog and horse food in the back cabinet. Rostoa was in the corner and had started to eat the potting soil from the plants and Eliana had ripped the top off the sink and was drinking the water as it sprayed out. Clerice was eating cake that she found in the trash, from two days ago! Huliona had torn the vegetable drawer out of the wall and was swallowing wads of bustle sprouts, whole!

"Oh um wait! Don't throw that! Ahh!" Throrta cried as she caught flying donuts, pizza and bread. Catton had taken cover under the table as the girls continued their raid.

"Hey Huliona!" Eliana cried her mouth full of pudding. "Catch!" Eliana launched a pomegranate across the room towards Huliona.

Huliona jumped into the air and caught the pomegranate. She took a huge bite, skin and all. "Thanks!" She cried.

Throrta looked astounded. Throrta then winced as she watched Rostoa swallow a rock and not notice. She then looked over at Cira, who had started frying eggs on her palm and eating them by the dozen.

Huliona had finished all the vegetables and fruit. She was now looking for mushrooms. Huliona pranced over to Catton. "Do you have any mushrooms?" she asked, her eyes shinning.

Catton couldn't help but smile and let out laugh. "Yes." He answered. "There are some in the back pantry."

"Show me!" Huliona cried excitedly.

Catton led Huliona into the back pantry. They soon disappeared among all the stored food. A minute later Huliona emerged from the pantry holding a mushroom about as big as her head. There was a huge bit taken out of it and Huliona was smiling and chewing contently.

Clerice laughed. "Enjoying that mushroom Huliona!?" Rostoa called between gulps of raw pancake batter.

A minute later Katrina walked in. She stopped for a moment then went about her business like nothing was wrong. Throrta hurried over to her. "Katrina!" she cried. Katrina looked up from her magazine. "What is going on!? Why are the Queens tearing apart my kitchen!?" Throrta cried exasperated. "It is a mad house in here!"

Katrina ducked as a turnip flew over her head. She then saw Hatara swallow nine crackers at once. "It's normal." She said plainly.

"What do you mean it's normal!?" Throrta cried. "It doesn't look normal to me!"

"Well they are supposed to be doing this." Katrina said. "A long time ago when King's and Queen's were nervous before a battle they normally would not eat. So because they did not eat they would get sick and not be able to fight. So a wise old wizard decided to put a spell on all the future King's and Queen's to make them want to eat, a lot. This way they would not get sick before battle." Katrina finished.

"Oh." Throrta said.

Katrina rose from her chair and walked over to Clerice who had started on the spaghetti from the night before. Latopa and Cira had joined her. "Okay," Katrina said. "You girls have had enough."

All the girls looked up, seeing Katrina for the first time. They ignored her and kept eating. Katrina sighed. She went over to Huliona and pried the mushroom from her hands. She then grabbed the bowl of spaghetti from Clerice and took the other food away from Eliana, Rostoa and Hatara. She ushered them all towards the door.

"But I'm still hungry!" Latopa wined as she was pushed out the double doors.

"No your not," Katrina said. "Trust me."

Soon all the girls were out of the kitchen and it was silent once more. Throrta sat down at the table and surveyed the mess the girls had left behind. Catton had started to pick up some of the food.

"How will I ever clean this!?" Throrta said.

Suddenly the double doors burst open again. Clerice ran into the kitchen, grabbed a donut, and ran out again.

****

Clover sat on the edge of her barge. Her long fiery tail flew out behind her in the wind. It was strange for a light person to be so close to water for they usually liked to be on plains where the sun was brightest. But Clover was different; she liked working near the water. She had always thought it interesting and different than light in a wonderful way. Although today Clover was not pondering about the waters secrets, she was waiting for Queen Cira. She hadbeen summoned by her this morning, all of her subjects had. Clover did not really know why. She figured it had something to do with the battle.

Clover heard a splash beside her in the water. She glanced at the waters shimmering surface and saw Warthon, her mer friend swimming towards her. "Hi Warthon." She said as he came up to the barge.

"Hi Clover." Warthon said as he put his arms up onto the barge.

"What are you doing here?" Clover asked.

"I was summoned by Queen Eliana." Warthon said. "All of the mertoids were. We were told to wait at the nearest patch of land or the nearest boat."

"I was summoned too." Clover said. "By Queen Cira."

"I bet it's about the battle." Warthon said. "I want to know when it is and how we will be fighting."

"Uhhh, I don't." Clover said. "I'm nervous. I've never fought a battle before."

"Me either." Warthon admitted. "But I'm sure we will be okay. Katrina has been training us and the Queens well."

"I know." Clover said. "But, well, I just wish we didn't have to fight at all!"

"Me too." Warthon sighed.

They looked up; Cira and Eliana were coming towards them. After Katrina had taken the girls from the kitchen they had all gotten dressed and sent to gather all the soldiers for the army, every single one. The girls knew this would take all day and were not looking forward to this task. So they made an announcement all throughout Etarfia telling the soldiers to go to certain places, this would make them easier to find. So they set out. Huliona would get her soldiers, Hatara hers Clerice hers and so on.

"Hello Clover, Warthon." Cira said. She was acting very serious and she looked a bit nervous. So did Eliana.

"Ya, hi guys." Eliana said.

"Greetings." Clover and Warthon said.

"Clover," Cira said. "I have come to tell you that the battle is tomorrow. You need to report to Silver Moss Hill behind the palace to get fitted for your battle armor and get your weapons."

"Yes Queen Cira." Clover said. "Right away." Clover then waved to Warthon and sped off towards Silver Moss Hill.

Cira then nodded to Warthon. She jumped onto Yotru's back and the two took off into the sky in search for more soldiers. Eliana approached Warthon.

"Hey." She said.

"Hello Queen Eliana." Warthon answered.

"Just call me Eliana!" Eliana said a little annoyed.

"But you are a Queen." Warthon said. "Don't you want to be addressed as one?"

"No!" Eliana said. "Before I came here I was just a regular girl. It's weird to be called Queen. So just call me Eliana."

"Oh, well okay." Warthon said with a smirk.

"What!?" Eliana said.

"Nothing!" Warthon said quickly.

"Anyway," Eliana said. "You also need to report to Silver Moss Hill, to get your weapons and armor."

"Sure thing." Warthon said. "See ya!" He then turned and swam off towards the river that ran along side Silver Moss Hill.

****

Eliana had been out all day looking for soldiers and telling them where to go for their armor. She was now swimming along the eastern boarder of the island. She had been in the ocean for hours gathering mertoid's, ice dwarves, water pixies, and so on. She hated this part of the ocean. It was completely deserted. The water was murky and there were extremely tall sea fans everywhere, you never know what could be lurking around the next bend.

Eliana swished her mertoid tail a little faster and swam lower to the ocean floor. She was scanning the sand ahead of her when she saw something gold glint in the dim light. Curious she swam over to the object. She recognized it to be a little gold chain sticking out of the sand. She grabbed it and pulled.

Eliana was not prepared to see what was on the other end of the chain. At the end was a small, oval, gold, mangled disk. Eliana instantly knew what it was. The disk looked like it had been hit with something. And in a pattern on the disk there were seven indents, it looked as though jewels had been in each one. Eliana took a deep breath of water in, she then slowly, ever so slowly held her wrist up to the necklace. It was the wrist with her silver bracelet and gem on it. She blew out the water in astonishment and realization. Her gem was the exact same size as the indents. She also noticed something else. When she had picked up the necklace she had felt some sort of tension in it. It was like the necklace was lonely or waiting for something. But when she put her gem next to it the tension seemed to subside, and the necklace felt relaxed. Eliana now knew, with no doubt in her mind, that this was the necklace from the story. This was the necklace that started everything.

The necklace Safferstar had smashed. The necklace that gave Eliana and the other girls their powers.

Eliana looked at the necklace for a long time; she wasn't sure what to do with it. Maybe the last owner did not know either for now it was at the bottom of the deserted part of the ocean. Eliana finally decided to keep it. She knew she couldn't just leave it here, if she found it other people could too.

Eliana was going to continue through the murky water when she saw Hatara flying in the air above her. Eliana swam to the surface. She popped her head out of the water.

"There you are!" Hatara said. "I've been," Hatara trailed off. "Are you okay? You look strange."

"Thanks!" Eliana said.

"No! I mean you just look worried." Hatara said.

"Ya, ya I know. I am worried." Eliana then held up the necklace for Hatara to see.

Hatara's face had a look of astonishment on it. "It, it's the necklace,"

"Safferstar smashed." Eliana finished.

Hatara took the necklace in her hands. She felt the tension, as Eliana had then she felt it ease when her staff and gem were put next to it. "How did it get here?" Hatara asked.

"I'm not sure." Eliana answered.

"We should keep it." Hatara said.

"We should. Who knows, it may help in a tough situation." Eliana said.

Hatara took the necklace and put it in the shoulder bag she was carrying. She then grabbed Eliana under the arms. She lifted her out of the water and the two flew off towards the palace.

****

Katrina tapped her foot impatiently as she waited for the seven Queens by the Lake Of Dreams and Sorrow. Finally she saw Cira flying in of Yotru. Hatara was close behind with Eliana. A minute later Latopa rode in on Nightin. Frina and Melark then arrived and told Eliana and Hatara the last of their soldiers had been gathered.

"Where are the others?" Latopa asked.

"Huliona is gathering up the last of the Frayed Ferins. Rostoa is rounding up the rock giants. And Clerice has gone to fetch the cloud griffins. Katrina said.

Then, as if on cue Rostoa and Shantoro arrived with five rock giants including Nison. There were not many in Etarfia for they were so big. Rostoa then sent them off to Silver Moss Hill. Next was Clerice with one hundred Cloud Griffins. And finally Huliona with two hundred Frayed Ferins, they were all sent to Silver Moss Hill.

The girls then all gathered around Katrina in the dimming light. "Girls," she said. "It's time." They all looked around at one another. "It is time to get ready for the battle, your hour has arrived."

The girls smiled. "Yes, our time has come." Huliona said.

"It really is the dawn of battle." Clerice said.

Chapter 35

ONLY THE MOON

Each Queen stood in her room looking at her battle armor. They were all afraid, but they knew the time had come to end the war with the evil witches, once and for all. Huliona took the skirt of her battle armor and held it up. She sighed and gave a little smile. She took the dress and slipped it on. Huliona then pulled her boots on.

Huliona walked over to her desk. She then started to pin up parts of her hair with rose thorns. Huliona also pushed small pink flowers into her hair. Huliona then weaved vines into the strands she had left down and curled them. She then put her sword belt made of bark on. Huliona turned to her sword.

Huliona had nestled her sword high in the leafy branches of her tree in the center of her room. Huliona shuffled her feet a little. Suddenly a large mushroom grew out of the floor where Huliona was standing. The mushroom lifted Huliona up to the top of her tree where her sword rested. Huliona took the sword and put it in the holder on her belt. She hoped she would not need to use it that much.

She stomped her feet on the top of the mushroom and it shrank to the floor. Huliona then walked over to her door.

She turned back to her room. She scanned it, a little sad. She looked at her bed, the soft leaf that she slept on every night, her tree and vanity.

"Thank you." She said. Huliona then walked into the hallway. "Oh!" Huliona cried. "You look stunning!"

"Thank you!" Eliana replied. "So do you!"

Huliona and Eliana were the only ones in the hall. Eliana had put her blue wrap dress and boots on. She had put her hair in the shell comb Colly had given her. Eliana had also put silver streaks in her hair. Her sword also hung around her waist.

Cira was the next to come out of her room. She had on her flowing yellow and orange dress. Her hair was down and she had put streaks of real gold in her hair. Cira had also polished her arm band and gem. Her sword handle was also very shiny and it hung on a woven belt around her waist. She had also put her shoes made of sunrays on.

Latopa was next. She had her rough maroon dress on and no shoes. But she had rubbed glitter on her feet to make them sparkle. She also had her sword and had put dark brown ties in her long wavy hair. Rostoa was the next to come out. She had her dark brown shirt and capri pants on. Rostoa had also put her soil shoes on and her sword belt. Rostoa had pulled her hair back into a bun and curls sprayed out of the center, light brown streaks also ran through her hair.

Next was Hatara. Hatara had her shorts and shirt on. She also had her violet shoes and her sword belt rested around her waist. Hatara's hair was completely curly and there were small crystals sprinkled throughout the curls. But the best thing was her wings. Her wings were their usual milky white but they glittered. The girls applauded when they saw them.

Last was Clerice. She had her gray hoop skirt dress on and her boots. Her hair was mostly down but the sides were held back with real lightning bolt clips, streaks of pink were also in her hair. Her sword also rested comfortably in her belt.

The seven girls looked around at each other, fear and confidence in their eyes, but also doubt.

"Can we do this?" Rostoa asked. "I mean have we taken on too much?"

"I hope we can do this." Latopa said. "Everyone else thinks we can."

"Exactly." Huliona said. "Which is why we should think we can do it too. Everyone out there is counting on us. Let's show them they didn't make a mistake bringing us here."

The girls all gave meek smiles. "Ready?" Hatara asked.

"Ready." Everyone said together.

All seven girls then joined hands and started down the marble stairs for what seemed like the last time. The things that had brought them here flashed through their minds. Huliona saying goodbye to her father as she climbed onto the ferry. Hatara and Eliana going out for a simple day of fun then being attacked by a leopard seal. Rostoa hearing the mysterious voice in her yard. The voice that turned out to have been with all the girls their whole lives. Cira finding Huliona and Latopa on the beach. Latopa losing her parents and brother. Clerice meeting Cira on the tour bus. All this seemed so far away yet so close as each Queen took a step down the stairs, closer to battle.

****

Katrina and Safferstar waited near the door for their Queens. As the girls approached a tear rolled down Safferstar's cheek.

"Oh! What is it?" Cira asked running to her.

"I'm just so proud of you!" Safferstar said looking around at all the girls. "You have come such a long way!"

The girls smiled and Cira hugged Safferstar.

"Okay," Katrina said. "We don't have all night."

The girls smiled. "Where have I heard that before?" Eliana said glancing at Safferstar.

"Oh ya!" Cira said "Safferstar said that to us when we were trying to decide if we should go to Etarfia or not!"

"Well you made the right choice now let's go!" Katrina said pushing all of them out the door.

"Oh my gosh!" Huliona cried.

"Wow!"

"Cool!"

All the girls cried with surprise as they stepped outside. All lined up along the Lake of Dreams and Sorrow were wagons made out of rough tree bark. They had no tops and each wagon had rows of benches with drawers underneath then. Many of the soldiers were already in the wagons for these were the wagons that were going to carry them to the battle field. Although some were not yet in, they were mostly generals making last minute checks on weapons and soldiers.

"Moyan!" Clerice cried.

All the girls looked up. Moyan was flying towards them with a huge smile on her face. "My Queens!" she cried, stopping in front of them. "My people!" Moyan moved aside.

Everyone's jaws dropped. Behind Moyan were thousands of pixies and fairies. There were petal pixies, moon beam fairies, ice fairies, all the types of pixies and fairies you could imagine.

"Moyan! This is amazing!" Latopa cried. "I can't believe it!"

Moyan blushed. "Thank you!" she said.

"Yes, this is wonderful!" Hatara said smiling. Hatara then told the pixies and fairies to go sit on the sides of the wagons.

Alrie, Huliona's horse then approached the girls. "Great Queen's of Etarfia, it is time for your speech." She said. Huliona then climbed onto Alrie's back. The other girls then climbed onto their power soul mates backs and they all approached the front of the wagon line. Katrina and Safferstar followed close behind.

"Etarfian's!" Katrina cried. "You must quiet for our Queen's are about to give their speech!"

Everyone instantly went silent. Nothing was heard throughout the palace yard. No one moved. Only the wind softly blew through the cool crisp night. Then all the Etarfian's in the wagons stood up and waited.

Huliona took a deep breath. "Etarfian's," she started. "Many years ago an evil was inflicted on your land. A deep evil that caused destruction and sadness."

"No land deserves this." Eliana said. "I have to say, when Safferstar came to us and asked for help we did not know if we were going to take up this task and responsibility of saving Etarfia."

"But we thought about it." Rostoa said. "We realized that we had to help, no matter what the dangers were or the problems. And trust me, we were scared at first."

"We didn't know if we could do it, or how." Cira continued. "We had problems on this journey, doubt, fear, and anger. But through all that, we had this feeling that we belonged in Etarfia."

"We knew we had to help you." Latopa said. "We knew you were counting on us, and believed in us. We knew you knew, from the very beginning, that we could save Etarfia and restore it to its former glory."

"That is exactly what we are going to do." Clerice said. "We will march into battle, confident and strong. The evil we face, will not stand a chance."

"For happiness, love, and hope is stronger than hate and lies." Hatara spoke up. "So, are you with us? Will you help us vanquish the evil witches! All the hate and anger that has surrounded you for so long?"

"Are you with us?!" Huliona shouted thrusting her fist into the air. A loud roar of approval rose from the Etarfian soldiers gathered around the lake. "So!" Huliona cried. "We ride to battle!"

****

The wagon wheels clattered along through the small forests, large fields and steep hills the Etarfian army was traveling. It was a clear night. There were no stars, only the moon shed its bright light on the seven Queens.

None of them had talked since they left the palace. Occasionally the wind would whisper words of encouragement to Hatara. Huliona felt the trees' comforts. But other than that, all the girls were engrossed in their own thoughts.

Finally, Latopa spoke. "Are you, afraid?" she asked.

"Afraid?" Huliona said.

"Of, of dying?"

Huliona and the others were silent for moment. None of them had really asked themselves if they were afraid they were going to die.

"During the battle?" Huliona asked, a little reluctant to answer the question.

Latopa nodded.

"Yes." Huliona finally said. "I'm terrified."

"So am I." Eliana said.

"I am afraid." Hatara said.

"Me too." Cira added sadly.

"Yes." Clerice said.

"Of course." Rostoa finished.

"Are you afraid?" Clerice asked Latopa.

"Very." Latopa said. "But, I have a feeling we will be okay."

"Ya," Eliana said gazing off in front of her. "me too."

"You needn't be afraid." Alrie said. "You are all strong warriors and you will do well in battle."

"Yes," Mrenshoon agreed. "You will do great."

"I hope your right." Hatara said. "I'm just so nervous."

"Do not be too nervous Hatara." Frina said "We will be here with you."

They all heard a noise behind them they turned to see Katrina riding up to the front of the line. Katrina was riding Floyd, Nathlene's horse.

"My Queens." She whispered. "We have reached the battle field. Look yonder."

The seven Queens looked in front of them, straining to see in the dark. All they could see was a thin line of trees, and beyond the trees, from what the girls could see, was flat expanse.

****

"I wonder if the witches have arrived yet." Cira said, straining ahead.

"Let me go check it out." Latopa said. She turned into a cat and climbed onto Nightin's antlers. She then sprouted eagle wings and took off into the night towards the battle field.

Latopa returned a minute later, her eyes wide and fearful.

"What did you see?" Huliona asked.

"It is a large field, larger than any we have ever seen." Latopa said. "Its covered in coarse yellow grass."

"Did the witches arrive yet?" Rostoa asked.

"I don't think so. It was really quiet and I couldn't see a lot." Latopa said. She then jumped back onto Nightin's back and turned back into a human once more.

All of them were dead silent as they approached the trees. All seven girls went on either side of a tree so they were all in a line facing the field. Hatara felt the airs hesitation. Huliona felt the nervousness of the trees around her. Cira took a deep breath and blew out. She could see her breath in the air. The huge field seemed completely deserted.

Rostoa road out with Shantoro onto the field a few yards away from the others. She scanned the horizon. Nothing. She motioned for the others to come out onto the field. They all came out onto the field with Rostoa and once the last girl stepped in line with the others, Flash!

"Ahh!" the girls cried.

All of them except Cira shielded their eyes. Then they looked back. A corner of the sun was peeking over the horizon, its bright rays streaming out into the night. Soon half the sun had risen, then the whole sun! Soon it was high in the sky. It was day.

The girls had never seen the Etarfian sun rise before. They could not believe their eyes. Their sun rose slowly. But the Etarfian sun rose fast, in a matter of seconds, it was in the sky. They stood there still in disbelief, staring at the sun. Then, they heard it. As if released from a spell, they all snapped back to reality, a horrid sound ringing in their ears, the sound of marching.

They listened harder. A whip cracked, creatures snarled. The girls were nervous; they had never really seen what type of creatures they were going to be fighting. They had seen the creatures in the dungeons but they were very few. Suddenly, the witch's army broke the horizon. The witches were in the middle, not in the front as the girls expected them to be.

"Cowards." Huliona whispered. "You won't even lead your army into battle yourself."

The witches stopped a ways onto the battle field and their army quickly got into formation. It was quiet once more. The Seven Queens of Etarfia called their army, already in formation, out onto the battle field. The seven Queens were in front and Katrina and Safferstar were close behind them. Rostoa looked back at Katrina who nodded.

Rostoa tapped Huliona on the shoulder. "It's time." She said.

"Rostoa," Huliona breathed. "I don't know if I can do this."

"Oh Huliona! You can! Was it not you who said Safferstar would not have come for us if she knew we would fail?"

"I know I said that, It's just, there are so many of them!"

"I know. And I know you are afraid, I'm afraid. I bet the whole army is afraid, even Katrina. I know you can do this."

"Rostoa."

"Yes?"

"You're not my cousin."

"What?"

"You are my sister."

"Your sister?'

"Yes. We have been through too much together to say we are just cousins."

"I think you are right." Rostoa said. She looked at Huliona and smiled. Huliona smiled back.

"Now," Huliona said. "I am ready."

Huliona turned back to the witches army. She then rubbed her hands together and laid them flat. Suddenly multicolored petals fell from the air and onto Huliona's palm. Eliana then rubbed her hands together. Rain fell down and formed a pool in her outstretched hands. Hatara then rubbed her hands together, a small wind tunnel formed on her palms. Next Rostoa rubbed her hands together. Soil from the ground snaked up into the air and settled on her palms. Clerice rubbed her hands together and a small lightning bolt coming out of a cloud formed. Latopa then rubbed her hands together and a small bone carving of a deer rested on her outstretched hands. Last was Cira. She rubbed her hands together and a few rays from the sun came down and formed a pool of light in her hands.

The girls all closed their eyes. Then they threw their things into the air. Like a magnet they were all sucked together. There was a flash of light as they all collided. A minute later something fell out of the sky and landed in Huliona's outstretched hand. It was a horn, made from all the objects the girls had had in their hands. On the horn were carvings of different things such as fish, flowers, birds, and clouds.

Huliona closed her eyes, she thought of her father, his smiles. His smile when she had won a race against all the boys in her village. His smile when she had done a particularly good drawing. Huliona's eyes flew open. She raised the horn to her lips and blew. The sound that erupted from the horn was clear and sweet yet strong and fierce. The wind picked up and carried the sound across the battle field, across all Etarfia! It rang through everyone's ears.

"Ahhh!!" Huliona started to scream. The others joined her; they took off towards the witches army who was running to meet them. Hatara, Cira, and Clerice took off into the air with the pixies, fairies, sprite kins, light people, tornado dwellers, cloud people and many more.

The two forces collided. The battle had begun.

Chapter 36: A Sea Of Hate

Eliana flew off Melark. She shot ice knives at the first creature that approached her. She drew her sword and struck another creature as it rushed towards her.

Just as Latopa had asked, Nightin bucked her off his back. Latopa turned into a wolf midair. An evil wolf sprung at her, the two met and Latopa fought viciously.

Katrina stood on Floyd's back and drew her sword. She struck an evil phoenix as it soared above her. She then did a flip off Floyd and landed right in front of Dase. Dase smiled and drew her sword. Katrina was the first to strike. Dase blocked her blow and pushed Katrina back. Katrina stumbled and fell, but she was quickly up again and fighting Dase. Katrina had managed to put a gash in Dase's arm but that was about it. Dase had slashed Katrina across the face but had not wounded her anywhere else. Katrina was tiring though. Dase fought fast and Katrina had to move at lightning speed to keep up with her.

Dase struck Katrina's hand. Katrina dropped her sword. Suddenly the air turned black and surrounded Katrina. It wrapped around her legs and when she struggled the black air only tightened its grip. Katrina fell. Then the air then wrapped around her arms so Katrina couldn't move at all. Dase raised her sword. But suddenly she got this odd look on her face, of terror and confusion. Dase was grabbing at her neck franticly, but nothing was there. Katrina watched just as confused as Dase had been. Then Hatara materialized out of thin air, her arm around Dase's neck.

Dase, realizing Hatara was there fought for air franticly. But no matter how hard she tried she could not pry Hatara's arm from around her neck. Then suddenly Dase flipped Hatara over her head. Hatara landed hard on her back next to Katrina. Dase's eyes widened when she saw the staff in Hatara's hands.

"So," she said. "The Queen of air and wind, my opposite." Dase smiled. "We meet at last."

"You're finished!" Hatara snarled sitting up.

"Oh!" Dase cried. "I beg to differ! There can only be one ruler of air and wind and that is going to be me!" Dase raised her sword ready to strike, then. "AHHHHH!!" Dase cried.

Hatara stood up and held her arms out in front of her, she clenched her fists. A long thick rope of air had wrapped around Dase's middle. Hatara started spinning Dase around and around. Then, abruptly Hatara released the air rope. Dase fell to the ground. The second Dase had been defeated the black magic surrounding Katrina disappeared. Katrina jumped up and rushed over to Hatara.

Hatara and Katrina hugged. "Thank you!" Katrina said.

Hatara just nodded, tears welling in her eyes.

"Oh! No tears!" Katrina said wiping them away. "You did it Hatara! There is one less evil Etarfia must defeat!"

****

"YA!!" Huliona cried as she saw Hatara defeat Dase. "WOW!" Huliona ducked as a sword swiped through the air.

Huliona looked up and her eyes grew wide. The swords holder was ten feet tall. The creature had the head of a wasp and the body of a man. Huliona shot vines from her hands and wrapped them around the creature's neck. She then jumped into the air and started swinging around and around the creature's neck wrapping the vines tighter and tighter, cutting off its air supply. The creature fell to its knees.

Hulona snapped her vine and landed face to face with the creature. She drew her sword and finished it with a slash. The creature turned to ashes right before her eyes.

"Latopa! Huliona! To the east! Make a barrier to the east!" Katrina was screaming.

Huliona looked to the east. Her eyes widened, a stream of new creatures were approaching the battle field. Swoosh! Something swooped down from the sky and grabbed Huliona around the waist.

"Ahh!" Huliona kicked and screamed.

"It's me!" Latopa cried over the noise below.

Huliona looked up. Latopa had turned into a small dragon and was flying to the east side of the battle field.

"You first." Latopa said as they approached the oncoming creatures.

Huliona thrust her hands up towards the sky. Ten huge mushrooms with thick stems burst from the ground. Huliona then moved her hands in a weave like manner; vines appeared and wove in and out of the mushroom stems. Latopa then flew down to the barrier. She sprayed fire onto the vines making them melt together. Latopa then flew to the ground and set Huliona down.

Just as Latopa was about to take off into the sky once more, WAM! Latopa was knocked clear out of the air. She hit the ground hard turning back into herself. The fall had knocked the wind out of her and she couldn't breath.

"I can't breathe!" she squeaked. "Help I can't breathe!" Latopa tried to shout but it came out nothing more than a whisper. Latopa was desperate.

Suddenly Hatara swooped down from the sky, an air bubble in her hand. Hatara shoved the air bubble into Latopa's mouth, forcing it down.

"Oh, thank you Hatara!" Latopa said.

"Look out!" Hatara shouted.

Latopa jumped to her feet and saw a sabberon running towards her. She had no doubt that he was the one who had knocked her out of the air. Furious Latopa turned into a huge jaguar and met the sabberon head on, feeling no fear.

The two clawed at each other viciously. The sabberon pinned Latopa down. He lunged for her neck. Latopa turned into a mouse and scuttled from underneath him. Latopa then turned back into a jaguar. Latopa then ran full force into the sabberon. The sabberon sailed through the battle field. He landed on a creature that was about to kill an Etarfian. The sabberon got to his feet and ran for Latopa. Latopa was ready. Just before the sabberon lunged Latopa got onto her back and flexed her long claws. When the sabberon jumped he landed on her claws.

Latopa gripped the sabberon's feet with her claws then flipped onto her side and slammed the sabberon onto the ground. Latopa quickly turned into a dragon and spewed the sabberon's legs with fire. They were burned badly; the sabberon could not get up. Latopa, tired and a little shaky turned back into herself. She walked over to the sabberon.

"Go on!" he snarled. "Kill me. Get it over with."

Latopa stared at him. "No." she said.

"What?"

"I am not going to kill you."

The sabberon looked confused. "But why?"

Latopa took a deep breath. "Knowing you were once good, I cannot kill you." Latopa looked up and saw Clerice not far off above her flying towards some creatures with Mrenshoon. "Clerice!" Latopa called.

Clerice swooped down on Mrenshoon. "Could you imprison him please?" Latopa asked.

"Certainly." Clerice said.

Clerice walked over to the sabberon and moved her hands over the air above him. Small ropes of grey cloud that had started forming in the sky snaked down and formed a dome over the sadderon. The cloud then hardened.

"Why didn't you kill him?" Clerice asked Latopa as she turned into a dragon and they both took off into the sky.

"Knowing he was once good, I just couldn't do it. It didn't feel right." Latopa answered. She then turned and looked behind her. "Clerice! Behind you!" Latopa shouted.

Mrenshoon whirled around. A creature with just back legs, wings and a head with razor sharp teeth was heading strait for Clerice. "Mrenshoon know!" Clerice cried. Mrenshoon bucked Clerice off his back. Clerice's legs turned into the bottom of a tornado, propelling her forward. As she approached the creature her arms turned to a dark grey fog, and then hardened. It looked like she had iron fists. Bam! Clerice crushed the creatures head in between her fists. The creature started falling. Clerice then shot a lightning bolt at the creature to finish it. The second the lighting bolt hit the creature it turned to ashes.

Clerise's arms and legs then turned back to normal and she started falling. Mrenshoon quickly caught her and flew back to Latopa.

"Let's go." Latopa said, and she and Clerice flew off into another mob of flying creatures.

****

Cira flew on Yotru's back. She soared through the battle field setting evil creatures aflame. Most of the creatures turned to ashes after a few minutes but a few managed to douse her flames.

"Drat!" Cira said as one of the particularly large creatures put out his flaming arm.

Cira was about to go for a sabberon directly below her when, WAM! A huge red fire ball hit her in the side, sending her flying off Yotru who was careening towards the ground. Cira landed in a crumpled heap on the ground. Furious she sprung to her feet.

"Yotru!" she cried. "Are you okay!?"

"I'm fine Cira." Yotru said as he stood up and shook himself off.

Cira, her eyes blazing then looked around, searching for who ever knocked her out of the sky. She then spotted her. A few yards away Braysip was standing neatly as a small rope of red fire twisted around her fingers.

"Yaaaa!!" Cira yelled as she engulfed herself in yellow flame. Braysip smiled and engulfed herself in red flame.

Cira sped towards Braysip, Braysip ran to meet her. The two flames met. Sparks flew everywhere as Cira and Braysip fought, soon the two were one huge ball of yellow and red flame. Every once in a while you would see someone throwing a punch or swiping their sword.

"Ahh! Uh!" Cira was thrown from the ball of fire. She landed on her back.

Braysip brought her sword down on Cira. Cira flipped onto her stomach, narrowly missing the blade. Cira then shot a ball of magma at Braysip. It hit Braysip in the chest. Braysip screamed and engulfed herself in red flame. She ran for Cira who met her head on. The two were once again, one big ball of fire. As Cira fought her fire grew hotter and her anger flared. Suddenly, there was a wave and Braysip was thrown from the fire ball, but her fire didn't follow. Braysip landed painfully on her side then whipped around to look at Cira. Cira had both her fire and Braysip's fire around her, and she looked just as confused as Braysip.

What Cira did not know was this, for exactly one second during her battle with Braysip she had been at her strongest. At that second she had grabbed Braysip's power band. When she did this she had sucked Braysip's power into her, leaving Braysip powerless.

Cira, realizing she now had twice the power she normally had looked at Braysip and smiled. Braysip, her eyes wide with fear turned to run. Cira flung a rope of Magma from her hand, it wrapped around Braysip's neck and pulled her down. Cira then flung herself into the air and mustered up all her power. Then, WAM! She brought her shoulder down hard on Braysip's back. Sparks flew. When the sparks settled Cira was lying on her back next to Braysip, who had been defeated.

****

Rostoa flung herself at Cira. She had seen the very end of the fight and was happy, but Cira looked hurt. Rostoa grabbed Cira under the arms and hoisted her up. Cira had started to open her eyes.

"Cira! Cira you did it! You defeated Braysip!" Rostoa was shouting.

"Wa," Cira mumbled. "I, I did?" her eyes were wide.

"Yes!" Rostoa shouted.

Cira looked down at Braysip. Suddenly the whole fight came flooding back to her. "I did! Oh Rostoa! I did!"

"Yes!" Rostoa laughed.

Suddenly the ground started to shake. "Are you doing that?" Cira asked looking over at Rostoa.

"No," Rostoa said. "I don't know what's doing it."

The two then heard the screams, the screams louder than all the others. They looked in the direction of the screams. A giant had stepped over Huliona and Latopa's barrier, it had blood red eyes. Rostoa and Cira's jaws dropped. They knew this was not one of their own.

****

Eliana had spotted the giant as well. She ran to Huliona who was nearby fighting an orge. Eliana formed an icicle in her hand. She struck the orge in the back, it turned to ashes.

"Thanks!" Huliona said.

"No problem." Eliana replied. "But he is!" Eliana pointed to the giant who was already causing great chaos.

Huliona looked over at Eliana. "Do you think...?"

"Yes." Eliana said.

"Are you sure?" Huliona asked. "We have only done that spell once."

There was a roar from the giant. "Yes I'm sure!" Eliana said. "Go get Rostoa."

Huliona jumped onto Alrie's back who had just rode up beside her. Alrie was about to suggest the spell herself. Alrie galloped through the crowd of fighting soldier's towards Rostoa.

"Rostoa!" Huliona cried as she rode up to her. "Its time."

"Really?" Rostoa asked, looking nervous.

"Yes."

Rostoa jumped onto Alrie's back with Huliona, the two then rode back to Eliana.

"Good luck!" Cira cried after them.

They finally reached Eliana. Rostoa and Huliona jumped off Alrie. They quickly linked hands with Eliana. The second they all joined hands an invisible shield formed around them, no creature could get to them. The three Queens then started to recite the spell.

"Shre las mera ro,

Coshn semis macan toll.

Rias masjinz creates meis,

Shieild…

Basa ita orin eil!"

Once they finished blue started to swirl around Eliana, green around Huliona, and brown around Rostoa. The columns grew taller and wider. Soon the columns of color disappeared. In the green columns place was Huliona, only she was much, much taller. Huliona was a giant tree person. In the brown columns place was Rostoa, she had turned into a rock giant. In the blue columns place was Eliana, only she was tall, very tall and completely made of ice.

Rostoa was the first to charge the giant. She grabbed him around the middle and knocked him to the ground. The giant threw Rostoa off him and tried to rise but Huliona was upon him. She wrapped a thorny arm around his neck and pulled the top half of him down again. Rostoa was up again. She jumped on the giants legs.

"Eliana! I can't hold on much longer!" Huliona shouted. "Finish it!"

Eliana started spinning around and around. Small snowflakes and chunks of hail joined her. Eliana then stopped short screaming, "Reomin Crasbit!" she thrust all the snow and hail towards the restrained giant.

The snow and hail at the front of the mob formed a sharp tip right before it hit the giant. When it hit the giant the creature turned to ashes instantly. The moment the giant disappeared Rostoa, Huliona, and Eliana all turned back into their normal selves. The spell only lasted until you defeated your enemy.

Eliana quickly said goodbye to Rostoa and Huliona, unknowing of the terrible thing that was going to happen next.

****

Eliana leaped onto one of the mushrooms that made up Latopa and Huliona's barrier. She looked out over the sea of creatures trying to break it down. She chuckled to herself; they will never break it down she thought. But just in case I should probably get rid of them.

Eliana mustered up all her power; she was going to need it for what she was about to do. She mustered up all the power she could until she was glowing dark blue, as dark blue as the ocean. She then put her arms above her head and thrust them towards the mob of creatures. Suddenly a huge wave from the ocean burst up and over her head. It crashed over the barrier and onto the evil creatures who were still trying to get into the battle.

Once the water had settled she froze the giant pool. The creatures were trapped in the

ice. Eliana fell to her knees that had taken all her strength.

"Wrong move." A clear but evil voice said.

Eliana jumped to her feet and whipped around, her heart caught in her throat. Joycore was standing only a few yards away. Eliana started to back up. Wait! She said to herself.

I am a Queen, not a coward! Eliana then took more steps toward Joycore than she had taken back and readied herself for a fight.

****

Joycore flung herself onto the ice, Eliana raced after her. Eliana flung balls of flaming water at Joycore, but they always landed right behind her heels, exploding into sparks.

"Ahh!!" Eliana cried.

Joycore had spun around and flung two knives at her. Eliana jumped into the air and flipped, narrowly missing the blades. She landed neatly on the ice.

"Oh," Joycore said, walking toward Eliana. "you're the water Queen aren't you?"

"Yes I am." Eliana answered.

"Hmmm, it's a pity. Krees may have wanted to finish you." Joycore said. "But I want to finish you more!"

Then Joycore started morphing. She turned into a giant blue snake with silver eyes. She then grew back and front legs. She was not a lizard and she was not a snake. She was almost a mix of the two. Joycore then ran towards Eliana.

Eliana thrust her hands forward. A pale sea foam green shot from them. The blast hit Joycore in the chest, sending her flying backwards. Eliana then drew her sword and ran after Joycore. Joycore was up again and running towards Eliana. Joycore jumped onto Eliana and pinned her down. Eliana had wedged her sword into Joycore's mouth and was pushing on it with all her might to keep Joycore back. Eliana screamed as Joycore dug her talons into her arms. Eliana swiped her sword along the inside of Joycore's mouth. Joycore screamed and flew off of Eliana.

Eliana jumped to her feet. She took four huge snowflakes with sharp points from her sword belt. She flung them at Joycore. The snowflakes cut Joysore's sides, deep. Eliana then drew her sword and ran to Joycore. She raised her sword to finish the witch off. Suddenly Joycores long tail whipped around and slashed Eliana across the middle. Eliana fell onto her back, her waist burning.

Eliana forced herself up. The front part in the middle of her dress was torn. The tare revealed a deep gash.

"You'll never make it!" Joycore hissed. "You'll die just like the rest!"

"No!" Eliana screamed. "I won't let you WIN! Prika Esrope!"Eliana cried throwing her hands forward.

Five long thick ropes of ice rose up around Joycore. Then with all her might Eliana brought her hands down hard on the ice. The ice ropes then fell, crushing Joycore. The witch was finished. Eliana smiled with relief. Eliana whirled around to face the battle field, searching for one of her friends. Her smile quickly faded.

****

Eliana saw Capsa string the arrow and let it fly. She saw it soaring through the air, she saw Hatara in its path.

There was no time. No time to warn Hatara, no time to push her out of the way, no time to shield her, no time. Only time to run. Eliana ran as fast as her legs could go. Tears stung her eyes as she thought about what she was going to do. She jumped down from one of Huliona's mushrooms, and was soon running across the coarse yellow grass of the battle field. She ran, getting closer, getting closer…

"ELIANA!!" Hatara screamed. "No Eliana no!" Hatara flew to her friend's side. She took Eliana's head and put it in her lap.

Eliana was breathing in short quick gasps; the arrow had pierced her heart.

"Oh Eliana!" Hatara sobbed. "I'm going to save you," she said. "You'll be okay." Hatara reached for the arrow.

"No." Eliana breathed pushing Hatara's hand away. "Its no use, I'm done."

"No Eliana!" Hatara cried, tears streaming down her cheeks.

"Hatara the arrow has pierced my heart, I can feel it."

"Please Eliana."

"Promise you will tell the others I love them. That they are like my sisters." Eliana said.

"Elia…"

"Promise!"

"I promise! I promise!" Hatara sobbed.

"And, if you guys ever do get home, when you go back to Greenland," Eliana wheezed. "Tell my brother I love him too. And let him know I didn't want it to be this way."

Hatara only nodded, too upset to speak.

Eliana gave a little laugh. "I'm glad." She said. "I'm glad that leopard seal attacked us Hatara. Because if it didn't I would not be here. I would not have met the others girls and I would not be here with you, saving Etarfia." Eliana gave a violent shudder and grabbed Hatara's hand. "I have a feeling," Eliana wheezed.

"Oh Eliana no!"

"that everything is going to be alright." Eliana whispered the last phrase. She then closed her eyes and squeezed Hatara's hand once, twice. Then Eliana's grip loosened, her arm went limp.

Eliana was gone. The last thing she saw were the tiny snow flakes that had started to fall and blanket the cold ground.

Chapter 36

THE SEVEN SISTERS

Clerice stood rooted to her spot, her eyes wide, unblinking. She had seen Eliana die in Hatara's arms. When she did, she felt as though her heart had broken in two. She scanned the battle field with fierce hungry eyes, searching for the evil witch that had killed Eliana. She spotted Capsa; she had the bow and arrow.

"NO!!!!!!!!!!!!!!!" Clerice started screaming.

As Clerice's cry became louder and louder she grew stronger. Clerice grew tall and smoky grey. From the waist down Clerice was a tornado. From the waist up her body was made of dark storm clouds, but it held its shape. Clerice's eyes were a bright yellow. She torpedoed towards Capsa.

Capsa was terrified. She stood right where she was and watched as Clerice approached her. She knew she had no chance against her.

"You DON'T touch her!!!!!!!" Clerice screamed.

Clerice then gathered all the power she had into her hands, power she didn't know she had. She then thrust her hands at Capsa; it was all her attacks at once. The attacks hit Capsa full force. The attacks sent Capsa flying back. She slammed into a tree then slid to the ground.

Clerice then turned back to normal and sank to the ground, sobbing as the battle raged on around her.

****

Ever since Katrina had saw Eliana die her mind had disappeared into a dark place she could not fight her way out of. She almost fought mechanically, unable to stop. Katrina knew that is was not anger that had driven Clerice to vanquish Capsa, but sadness, a broken heart and pure grief. She was glad Eliana had been avenged.

"UHH!" Katrina was socked in the stomach by an evil creature.

Then suddenly Katrina saw a shiny black boot flying through the air. She was kicked in the face. Katrina hurtled to the ground, dropping her sword in the process. She winced as she turned over onto her back. Her jaw had broken and her lip was bleeding, she also had a nasty bruise on her stomach. Katrina sat up. Then her face went pale and her eyes wide.

"Ellow Katrina! Long time no see!" A gruff voice said.

"No," Katrina whispered under her breath, inching backwards.

In front of Katrina was a man. He had pale white skin and dark brown hair that went down past his shoulders. He had a dark purple cloak on and boots than reached his knees. The man smiled, displaying his perfectly white teeth.

Katrina gulped and mustered up all her courage. "What are you doing here!?" she shouted. "You were banished from Etarfia! Even the witches agreed to it!"

"Have the witches ever been very reliable?" He hissed, stepping closer. "I made a deal with the witches. A deal they just couldn't refuse."

"What deal was that?" Katrina spat, grabbing a knife a few inches away.

The man drew his sword. "To get ride of you!" he snarled. "Now, how would you like to die? Oh wait! That choice isn't yours!" The man laughed.

"It is my choice!" Katrina cried jumping to her feet. "I choose not to die!" Katrina hurled the knife at the man.

The man jumped aside, narrowly missing the blade. He looked at her and wagged his finger mockingly. He then swiped his sword through the air and sliced Katrina across the chest.

"Ahh!!" Katrina screamed, she clutched her chest in pain and fell to her knees. The man walked over to Katrina and grabbed her by the shirt. He lifted her off the ground so she was eye level with him.

"Word of advice wife!" he hissed. "Never challenge me! You will loose!" He then threw Katrina from his grip.

Katrina landed hard on her shoulder. She heard a cracking sound. "Ahh!!" Katrina shrieked.

"Finish her." Petorix, Katrina's husband said to the creatures creeping up behind him. The creatures surged forward.

Then against Katrina's own judgment, all she believed in, Katrina did the unthinkable. She got up and ran. She ran as fast as her legs would carry her. She franticly scanned the battle field for anyone that could help her, but there was no one. She could also feel the breath of the creatures on the back of her neck.

Katrina flew into the eastern forest. She started running down and old path in between the trees, the wind whipping by her face. Katrina stumbled; she tripped on a tree root. Katrina's cheek hit the cold ground. She tried to jump up again but she couldn't! She tried moving her legs but she couldn't! No matter how hard she tried. Katrina gave one last attempt to rise! It was no use, Katrina was finished. Katrina heard the creatures snarling, she heard their heavy feet pounding against the ground, getting closer. The creatures were upon her! Katrina closed her eyes.

****

Huliona was doing marvelous. She was vanquishing creatures on the spot! They didn't even have time to draw their swords. She was now fighting a particularly large goblin. Huliona blocked one of his blows. The goblin sliced his sword through the air, grazing Huliona's cheek. Furious Huliona struck the goblin in the stomach, turning it to ash. Huliona wiped the blood from her cheek.

She looked up; Acrim was standing near her staring at her and smiling. Huliona smiled and walked up to Acrim. Huliona stuck her face in Acrim's.

"Hi! I'm Huliona!" she said. "Prepare for your evil to end!"

Acrim's face twisted with rage, but surprisingly she calmed herself. "Hello. I am Acrim."

"I know."

"Your comment is a lie, for your magic will be the one to end."

"So, are you ready to die?" Huliona asked.

"The question is my dear, are you?" Acrim said.

Huliona drew her sword with powerful force. Then she heard something, a noise like, gasping. Huliona turned and looked behind her, she gasped. Moshtic had been standing behind Huliona, obviously waiting for the signal from Acrim to kill her. But when Huliona had drawn her sword she had accidentally struck Moshtic, the blow had finished her.

Huliona turned back to Acrim who was red with fury. Acrim drew her sword and thrust it toward Huliona. Huliona blocked the blow. The two fought with expert skill, blocking blows and just as powerfully, giving them.

"You know." Acrim said as they fought. "You and I seem very similar."

Huliona was silent. She too had noticed that as she fought Acrim they had similar techniques. But there was one big difference.

"No!" Huliona said. "You are full of lies, hate and evil! I am not!"

Acrim, furious, threw a punch. She hit Huliona in the nose, breaking it.

Huliona was thrown backward. She did a backwards tumble salt and landed on her feet. She stood up. Huliona's hand flew to her seed pouch. She grabbed three of the biggest seeds.

"Cacti crunch!" Huliona shouted flinging the seeds into the air towards Acrim.

As the seeds flew through the air they turned into three huge green spheres. Foot long spikes grew out of each. Two of the spheres hit Acrim's arm, giving her deep cuts. The third stuck into her legs. Her face twisted with pain Acrim pulled the cacti ball from her legs.

Huliona acted quickly, she turned her arms and hands into two long platinum mushrooms. Her hand was the top of the mushroom and her arm was the stem. Huliona punched Acrim in the forehead, then the side. She went for Acrim's face again, but just before she hit her, Acrim grabbed Huliona's arm.

Acrim whipped Huliona round and smashed her into a tree. Huliona rose but Acrim was ready. Acrim slashed Huliona's forehead. Huliona stumbled back. Acrim then slashed her thighs.

"Ahh!!" Huliona finally cried out in pain.

Huliona fell forward. Acrim caught her head; she took the hilt of her sword and smashed it against Huliona's temple. Acrim let Huliona fall to her knees.

"Did you really think you could win!?" Acrim cackled. "Foolish, foolish, foolish. You are just a kid. Here's some advice for your next life, never take on a job you can't handle."

Acrim then took her sword and plunged it into Huliona.

"Huuu…" Huliona felt an unbelievable pain shoot through her. She clenched her teeth.

Instead of looking at Acrim, smiling down at her wickedly, Huliona looked up at the sky. The snow flakes that had started to fall suddenly fell faster. Huliona then looked around. Her heart caught in her throat, she saw Eliana. She saw her friend laying on the ground, pale, her eyes closed an arrow in her chest. Huliona's heart burst! It seemed to leave her completely! Huliona could not even feel the pain anymore. Her tears, her green tears had started to melt the snow. Huliona's head reeled and her vision started to blur. Huliona then saw Rostoa, who had seen her too. Rostoa was fighting furiously, trying to get to her. Huliona then felt herself falling. Her cheek hit the cold earth. The snow seemed to seep into her skin. She saw Rostoa again, she was with her! Then…

Nothing.

****

Rostoa's mind reeled as she threw evil creatures aside, trying to get to Huliona. It was as if she had found an unbelievable strength inside her, stronger than the super strength she already had, a strength that had been just waiting to explode and finally did.

Rostoa was almost to Huliona, Oh! She saw her cousin, her sister fall. Fall onto her stomach! Rostoa was at Huliona's side; she drew her sword and struck Acrim hard, right in the side! Acrim had not been ready for the blow. Huliona had already beaten her up bad, so she was in utter shock when Rostoa's blade met her skin. Acrim fell.

Rostoa grabbed her hair before she hit the ground completely, she help Acrim up. Rostoa looked Acrim straight in the eyes.

"You killed my best friend and my family." She snarled. "Now, I'm going to kill you!" Rostoa then took her sword, and finished Acrim.

Rostoa walked up beside Huliona, brown tears streaming down her cheeks. She knew Huliona was gone. She was about to stoop down, when she felt something warm running down her back. Was it snow? No snow was cold. Rostoa reached her hand around to her back. She then brought it back around, but she never had time to look at it.

****

It was over quick for Rostoa. She then felt the pain shooting up and down her back; it then spread to her arms and legs, then her chest. Her vision turned blurry then went black. Then Rostoa couldn't hear. She was in a sightless soundless world. Rostoa fell. She fell across Huliona's back and the second her back touched Huliona's, her heart stopped.

****

Krees smiled. Her shot had been true. The knife she had thrown had hit the Queen of rock and soil right in the back. She strode up to where Huliona and Rostoa lay. She grimaced at the scene. Krees looked down, she spotted Rostoa's crown with her gem on it, she reached down to pick it up.

"Your highness." A gruff voice said.

Krees stood up. A sabberon was in front of her. "What? What do you want?" she snarled.

"More Etarfian's are coming from the north, orders?"

Krees looked at the sabberon, its eyes were different from the others, they were not their usual chocolate brown, full of hate. They were a greenish blue, full of sadness.

"Oh, um, uh…" she stuttered. "Uh,"

"Orders your highness!" the sabberon snarled, in a girl's voice!

"Ahhh!!" Krees screamed. The sabberon pounced. It grabbed her around the middle.

The sabberon bit down. It then threw her. Krees skidded across the ground for at least one hundred feet! The sabberon walked up next to Krees, and then turned into who she really was, Latopa Queen of Etarfia!

"You hurt my friends you pay the price!" she snarled, crimson tears streaming.

"You, you tricked me!" Krees wheezed.

"That was the idea!" Latopa said. Latopa then drew her sword. "Wait." She said putting it away. "You deserve a long painful death! For all the pain, evil, and destruction you have caused!"

Latopa then walked away from Krees, towards Huliona and Rostoa. Then only minutes later the last evil witch of Etarfia was dead.

****

The battle was nearing an end. Safferstar gathered groups of Etarfian's, led by Catton, to chase down what was left of the evil witches army. Soon all was quiet on the battle field, not a soul in sight. Except for Safferstar the Queen's and the falling snow.

Latopa scooped up Eliana in her ape arms. She brought her over to the others and laid her next to Rostoa. The arrow, knife and sword that had taken the three Queens' lives were gone. Now they just lay, side by side.

Cira leaned down. She made it so the three Queens were holding hands. She then sat down and grabbed Huliona's cold hand and wrapped it in her own. Clerice then sat down and took hold of Cira's hand. Latopa then took Clerice's hand and Hatara took Latopa and Eliana's hands. They all closed their eyes.

Suddenly Hatara's eyes flew open. She broke hands with Latopa and went over to Eliana.

"I don't know if this will help." She said reaching into Eliana's dress pocket. "But just in case." Hatara had taken out the necklace.

All the girls immediately knew what it was, but didn't say anything. Hatara placed the necklace in the center of their circle. She then took Latopa's and Eliana's hands once more. It was deathly silent as the snow and wind whipped at all their faces.

Suddenly Cira's eyes widened. "Guys! Huliona is glowing!" she shouted.

All attention turned to Huliona, she was! Huliona had started to glow green!

"Eliana is too!" Clerice exclaimed.

Eliana had started to glow blue!

"So is Rostoa!" Latopa cried out.

Yes! Rostoa had started to glow brown! The girls then noticed they had started to glow too! Hatara was glowing white, Latopa crimson, Cira yellow, and Clerice grey! Their glows grew brighter and brighter. They had to close their eyes the glows were so bright! Safferstar fell back ward and shoved her face into her hands, but even that could not shut out the light!

Suddenly small pieces of every girls glow shot into the seven indents in the necklace. The necklace then started to repair! The rust disappeared, and the disc smoothed out. It looked like it had been the day it was brought to Etarfia! Then the glows around the girls started to morph. They twisted in and out of each other so each girl had a piece of one of the other girls glow around her. Then there was a great pressure in the air. All the weight in the world seemed to be pressing on Etarfia! Suddenly the weight lifted. All the glows were sucked into the necklace. The necklace flashed a brilliant gold, then, everything was as it should be. It was all back to normal as if nothing had happened.

The girls opened their eyes and looked around. "What happened?" Hatara asked.

"Look!" Clerice called out pointing to Huliona, Eliana, and Rostoa's gems. They were all teeming with life. Streaks of color were running through them.

Then, "AHHH!!!!!" the girls screamed in surprise.

Huliona was moving! She had slowly opened her eyes and was now sitting up! Next was Eliana! Then Rostoa sat up! The girls screamed with happiness and careened towards their friends.

They attacked them with hugs, happy tears streaming from everyone's eyes. Eliana, Huliona, and Rostoa just realizing what had happened started crying too and hugging with all their might. After they had all stopped hugging and crying they stood up, wiping tears from their eyes.

Safferstar slowly walked up to Eliana, Rostoa and Huliona. Her eyes were huge and glassy, brimming with tears. "I, I thought I had lost you!" she sobbed.

"No!" Huliona said. "You will never loose us! Not again. We will always be here." Then all three girls wrapped Safferstar in a huge hug.

They all stood wiping tears from their eyes once more, laughing. "OOOO!!" Clerice said.

"It's delightfully cold out!"

"Oh yes." Safferstar said. She snapped her fingers. Seven cloaks each the color of the girls' gems appeared. The girls thanked Safferstar and put them on.

"Hey," Rostoa said looking around. "Where is Katrina?"

The others looked around too. "I haven't seen her since the beginning of the battle." Hatara said.

Worry and panic spread across all their faces. "Okay," Safferstar said. "No one panic, let's look for her. Also, look for wounded Etarfian's." They all agreed and set out.

Most of the girls went in pairs, but Huliona went alone, she needed to think. Huliona scanned the snow in front of her for any movement, but there was none. So, she kept trudging through the snow, hearing her friends calling for Katrina in the back round.

Then, she saw it, a figure walking through the snow towards her. Was it Katrina? No, from the waist down it looked too poofy, like a dress. Catton? Defiantly not. Huliona squinted harder through the snow.

"Mom?"

To be continued.

Would you like to see your manuscript become a book?

If you are interested in becoming a PublishAmerica author, please submit your manuscript for possible publication to us at:

acquisitions@publishamerica.com

You may also mail in your manuscript to:

**PublishAmerica
PO Box 151
Frederick, MD 21705**

We also offer free graphics for Children's Picture Books!

www.publishamerica.com

CPSIA information can be obtained at www.ICGtesting.com
Printed in the USA
BVOW07s1834261213

340166BV00001B/242/P

9 781462 690886